SORRY TO BOTHER YOU

A SCREENPLAY BY

BOOTS RILEY

MCSWEENEY'S

SAN FRANCISCO

McSWEENEY'S
SAN FRANCISCO

www.mcsweeneys.net

Copyright © 2014 Boots Riley

COVER AND INTERIOR ILLUSTRATION: Matt Taylor.

Printed in Michigan at Thomson-Shore.

ISBN: 978-1-944211-62-2

McSweeney's and colophon are registered trademarks of McSweeney's, an independent publisher based in San Francisco. McSweeney's exists to champion ambitious and inspired new writing, and to challenge conventional expectations about where it's found, how it looks, and who participates. McSweeney's is a fiscally sponsored project of SOMArts, a nonprofit arts incubator in San Francisco.

Kind people, I require your assistance.

This screenplay is my last hope for retribution against a godforsaken industry. I warned the parties involved that I would return, tenfold, the pain they have inflicted on me.

McSweeney's has forced me to change the names of all those mentioned so that they themselves may escape a lawsuit, but know that everything herein—every scene, every character, every word—is true. There is no exaggeration to be found here, no farce, no satire, no sarcasm. If there is humor, it is only because you find the sad and terrifying state of humanity humorous. If there is fantasy, it is only because you are a person who pushes experiences that you have not yet had into the realm of the unreal. But it is not my place to judge.

You will understand the dire situation I now find myself in once you have read this account. The forces exposed in the following pages are not as nice as they seem on television. There have been offices burgled, laptops stolen, journalists disappeared, fashion trends twisted into terror campaigns, and, of course, the thing you all have heard about, of which I told my editor I wouldn't speak. They will stop at nothing to make sure that this script never becomes a feature film.

Please do anything you can to help publicize this account. If you know any Hollywood executives, slap the banana daiquiri out of their hand, shove this in their face, and tell them that the human race is counting on them. If you happen to be a Hollywood executive, I'll buy you another banana daiquiri at a later date.

With all possible optimism, considering the circumstances,

Boots Riley
June 2, 2014

{*Since this screenplay was originally published in 2014,* Sorry To Bother You *has become a feature-length film, produced by Annapurna Pictures.*}

MAIN CAST

CASSIUS GREEN

MR. ANDERSON

DETROIT

SERGIO

JOHNNY

SALVADOR

MIKE

LANGSTON

DIANA DEBAUCHERY

SQUEEZE

FANCY SUIT GUY

FANCY SUIT GUY'S ASSISTANT

BENJAMIN ELLMAN

STEVE LIFT

INTERIOR — MANAGER'S OFFICE

A young man, CASSIUS GREEN, *is being interviewed for a job at a telemarketing firm. The interviewer looks over a lengthy résumé. In his lap,* CASSIUS *proudly holds a large plaque with the words* EMPLOYEE OF THE MONTH—CASSIUS GREEN *engraved on it.*

ANDERSON: Wow. You've really gone the extra mile by lugging that in here.

CASSIUS: Yes, sir. That's my style.

ANDERSON: Admirable. Your résumé is startlingly impressive as well. Most people just fill out the application. You were actually the manager of the Rusty Scupper restaurant for five years.

CASSIUS: (*Grinning*) Yes.

ANDERSON: Then you worked as a teller for Bank of America for two years, from '04 to '06, with a six-month overlap with the restaurant.

CASSIUS: (*Still grinning*) Mmmhmm.

ANDERSON: Oh! And it says here . . . you were employee of the month.

(CASSIUS *makes a Vanna White–style hand motion toward his plaque.*)

ANDERSON: What's that trophy in the bag there?

CASSIUS: Oakland High Moot Court Champion. I'm a salesman at heart.

ANDERSON: Intriguing . . . Mainly because I was bank manager at that particular B of A from 2003 to 2005. And you, Mr. Green, never worked there. I also called the number you gave for The Rusty Scupper. Was that your friend Salvador's number?

(CASSIUS *nods.*)

ANDERSON: The same Salvador who also applied here?

(*CASSIUS sees SALVADOR through the window, giving a thumbs-up.*)

CASSIUS: (*Forlorn*) I didn't know he applied too.

ANDERSON: It would've been smart if his outgoing message didn't say, "I'm Sal, bitches." So that plaque and the trophy? Did you steal them?

CASSIUS: Made them. Well, had them made . . . I just—I just really need a job.

ANDERSON: All right, Cassius Green. Listen. This is te-le-mar-ket-ing. We ain't fuckin' mappin' the human genome or finding fucking alternative fuel sources so that the hordes of flesh we call humanity can prolong their lonely existence. No. So I don't care whether you have work experience. I figure if you want to work at this craphole of a place, you must have nowhere else to go anyway. I'll hire damn near anybody. That bootleg plaque proves two things I need to know: you have initiative and you can read. You will call as many contacts as you can during your shift, and you will read the script that we give you. And you will show up to work tomorrow. Happy.

CASSIUS: Thank you, Mr. Anderson.

(*ANDERSON throws a training script, a small pamphlet of papers, in CASSIUS's lap.*)

ANDERSON: Cassius, one more thing. Stuss.

CASSIUS: (*Confused*) Stuss?

(*Without looking at it, ANDERSON points to a big butcher-paper sign on the wall that reads S.T.T.S. = STICK TO THE SCRIPT!, written in marker.*)

ANDERSON: Stuss. S.T.T.S. Stick to the Script.

INTERIOR — CASSIUS'S STUDIO APARTMENT

CASSIUS and his girlfriend, DETROIT, lie in bed in a very small studio apartment. On the nightstand there is a faded sepia-tone 1980s photograph of a sharply dressed man posing in front of a Lincoln Continental. The man has a very proud expression on his face. CASSIUS stares at the ceiling while DETROIT lays her head on his chest.

CASSIUS: Hey, Detroit. Do you ever think about dying?

DETROIT: Yeah, sometimes.

CASSIUS: I'm not talking about dying right now, like in an accident or something. I mean like when we're old. Like ninety. I think about it all the time. What will I have done that's important, that matters?

DETROIT: I just want to make sure that when I die I'll be surrounded by people who love me and who I love back.

CASSIUS: What about when those people die?

DETROIT: What do you mean?

CASSIUS: I mean at some point we're gonna die, our kids and grandkids are gonna die. Their kids. At some point, no one will even know you existed. There won't even be a record. At some point all life will end on this planet and in billions of years the sun will explode. None of this will have mattered.

DETROIT: Baby, it will always matter. Because it matters now. This moment, all of these moments. When I kiss you, it's not for posterity's sake.

CASSIUS: Spoken like a true artist. I mean, you found your calling, your reason. Your art. It matters to you. I feel like I'm just a hamster on a wheel. Like I'm just doin' shit to keep busy and stay alive. Till I die.

DETROIT: You'll find your calling, Cash. When we were in high school, you were the smart one, the funny one—

CASSIUS: Yep. What a disappointment—

DETROIT: Ay. Stop. You missed your cue back there. I said . . . When I kiss you, it's not for posterity's sake. That's when Cassius is supposed to kiss Detroit. Always seize the moment.

(DETROIT *kisses CASSIUS.*)

CASSIUS: Oh. So, you're another one of them "Stick to the Script" muthaf—

(DETROIT *interrupts him with another kiss and the couple begins to make out. All of a sudden, the wall abruptly swings upward—we see, for the first time, that this studio apartment is really a semi-converted garage, bordering the sidewalk—leaving the romantic couple exposed to the street and passersby.*)

DETROIT: Fuck, Cassius! I thought you fixed that!

CASSIUS: My landlord was supposed to.

STREET VOICE: (*Offscreen*) Get a room!

CASSIUS: Muthafucka, I *got* a room!

(CASSIUS *pulls the garage door closed, secures it, then sits back down on the bed. DETROIT gets up and walks toward the bathroom.*)

DETROIT: I gotta get to work anyway . . . Don't you start work today?

CASSIUS: Yeah.

(DETROIT *walks offscreen to the bathroom.*)

CASSIUS: If you want a second job, they said they hire anybody. You could try part-time.

(No answer from DETROIT. CASSIUS turns on the TV and sits back down. A commercial starts up.)

MAN ON TV: Everyone is talking about the WorryFree solution! And they should, because WorryFree is the revolutionary new business and lifestyle model taking the world by storm! We've got the answer for today's business climate and the answer for *you*!

DETROIT: *(Offscreen)* What are they paying you?

(CASSIUS is transfixed by the TV.)

MAN ON TV: When you sign a WorryFree contract, you guarantee yourself employment *and* housing for life! Stop worrying, get WorryFree! The WorryFree living quarters are state of the art.

(TV shows a chic-looking room with six bunk beds, like a prison done up by a hip interior decorator.)

MAN ON TV: The WorryFree food is to die for.

(TV shows a gigantic dining room with thousands of people in uniforms at long tables with chandeliers hanging overhead.)

MAN ON TV: And WorryFree careers are fulfilling and satisfying! Call 1-800 . . .

DETROIT: *(Offscreen)* Cash baby, what are they paying you?

CASSIUS: *(Staring at TV)* Uh, I think it's just commission. You ever thought about that WorryFree shit?

DETROIT: Are you crazy?

CASSIUS: (*Still staring at TV*) What, for working on commission? (*Looking up at* DETROIT) Nice earrings.

(*We see now that* DETROIT'S *oversize earrings are big, two-dimensional, gold metallic block letters. Her right earring reads* MURDER, MURDER, MURDER *and her left one reads* KILL, KILL, KILL.)

EXTERIOR — CASSIUS'S STUDIO APARTMENT

CASSIUS *exits his apartment through the side door and locks it. He is spotted by his landlord,* SERGIO, *who is wearing a necklace with an oversize gold cross, which has a Jesus with a frightfully pained face. This particular Jesus seems to be screaming and writhing in agony.*

SERGIO: Ay, Cash! I got overdue house notes, dude. How much longer do I have to wait for my money?

CASSIUS: Hey, Serge. I got a job now. I start today, so I'll have your money soon.

SERGIO: Damn, man. It's four months late now. It's like *soon* is your favorite word. That's the only fuckin' word I hear from you.

CASSIUS: Okay. I'm four months late with the rent. But you should be ashamed. This land was created—by God—for the people and the animals to live off of, but greedy people like you horde it for yourselves and your families and charge the rest of us for the right to live on it.

SERGIO: Me and my family? Cassius, I'm your fucking uncle. The bank might take my fucking house. Four fucking months. I gave you the car you're driving.

CASSIUS: It's a damn bucket!

SERGIO: Oh yeah? Give it back then! No? That's what I thought. That car is better than your shoes. I need my money in two weeks, asshole. This time I mean it.

EXTERIOR — GAS STATION

CASSIUS *drives his car to the gas station. It's a red 1982 Honda Civic with a gray primered hood and doors. The car is very loud—maybe missing a muffler—and has steam coming from the radiator.* CASSIUS *walks to the cashier's window.*

CASSIUS: (*Through window*) Gimme forty on two!

(CASHIER *looks down at the forty cents* CASSIUS *has left and looks back at* CASSIUS *and the car disapprovingly.*)

CASHIER: (*To himself*) That's a damn bucket.

EXTERIOR — SHOT OF OAKLAND

CASSIUS *drives through the city. He passes a group of adult men playing football. They are wearing Oakland High School jerseys, but they are obviously not in high school—some of them have beards, others have beer guts.* CASSIUS *honks his horn rapidly and repeatedly as he passes. They all look. Many wave.*

VARIOUS FOOTBALL PLAYERS: Ay, Cash! What up?!

CASSIUS: (*Yelling, sing-song*) O-High Play-ers!

(CASSIUS *gives the clenched-fist-pull acknowledgment and keeps driving. He passes a mural-size street-level billboard that shows a side view of a five-bed bunk bed with people in each bed. They all look very comfortable. Two of them are sleeping.*

One of them is reading a book. Another is laughing while watching television on a small screen in his bunk. And then there is one in the middle, smiling widely, looking straight into the camera, giving a thumbs-up. The caption reads WORRYFREE. IF YOU LIVED THERE, YOU'D BE AT WORK ALREADY!*)*

INTERIOR — OFFICE BUILDING LOBBY

CASSIUS *enters the office building. As he walks toward the telemarketing offices, he sees a* MAN IN A FANCY SUIT *use a key to summon an elevator. The elevator doors are gold, with hieroglyphics on them—1920s-era faux-Egyptian style. When the elevator opens we see velvet-upholstered walls and a chandelier. This is a ridiculously luxurious and gaudy elevator. There seems to be a purple glow emanating from inside. The* MAN IN A FANCY SUIT *smiles at* CASSIUS *while entering the elevator. Cassius seems puzzled, but continues on his way to work.*

INTERIOR — TELEMARKETING CUBICLES

CASSIUS *is led into a room where a racially mixed group of about one hundred people sit at cubicles: blacks, East Asians, South Asians, Latinos, and whites. Many of the white callers look "punk." Leading him:* JOHNNY, *wearing shirt and tie. His face is tattooed and he has a Mohawk.*

JOHNNY: This is where the magic happens. Clock in here and grab a seat wherever you want. Have you studied the script?

CASSIUS: Yeah.

JOHNNY: Good. I'm just gonna let you get started, then.

*(*CASSIUS *sits at a cubicle. He takes out a photocopy of the picture from his nightstand and tacks it to the wall.)*

JOHNNY: Look, I can be your best buddy, or I can be an asshole. Clock in, don't be lazy, hit your contacts, and bring in some money, and I won't have to be an asshole. If you do real good, eventually you might be able to be a Power Caller.

CASSIUS: What's a Power Caller?

(*JOHNNY points at the ceiling.*)

JOHNNY: Up there. That's where the callers are ballers. Where they make the real money. They have their own elevator.

CASSIUS: Oh yeah, I saw that.

JOHNNY: (*Walking away*) And stick to the script.

(*CASSIUS puts the headset on and clicks the computer keyboard. A name pops up and we hear a phone ring. The phone picks up. We see a split screen. In the other frame: a man sitting at a dinner table with his family. He looks annoyed.*)

PERSON ON PHONE: Yello.

CASSIUS: (*Reading script in a very stiff manner*) Um, Mr. Davidson. Sorry to bother you, my name is Cassius Gr—

(*Phone hangs up.*)

(*Another name flashes on the screen and we hear another ring. Split screen with a woman and a man on a couch, naked, ready to have sex.*)

PERSON ON PHONE: Hello?

CASSIUS: Hi, Mrs. Slater! I'm Cassius Green. Sorry to bother—

(Phone hangs up.)

(Name flashes on screen and phone rings. We see a split screen of a woman sitting at a table in a darkened kitchen. She looks very sad.)

CASSIUS: Hello? Hey! Mrs. Costello!

WOMAN ON PHONE: Yes?

(CASSIUS looks up at a banner that says STICK TO THE SCRIPT! He then looks at the script, which says: 1. Introduce yourself. Be their friend.*)*

CASSIUS: This is Cassius Green. I'm with Insight Encyclopedias and I know you've enjoyed our Insight Bird-Watching books, so I just wanted to help you out—

WOMAN ON PHONE: I'm sorry, young man, we don't have any money. My husband is in the hospital . . . he's seventy-three with stage-three cancer and we—

(MRS. COSTELLO continues, starting to sob.)

(CASSIUS looks at the banner, then down at his script. He flips frantically to the middle of the pamphlet: 5. Make any problem a selling point. For example, use this language: "Well, Mr. Smith, it's interesting that you say that because . . . "*)*

CASSIUS: Well, Mrs. Costello, it's—it's interesting that you say that because book number five in the Insight series is all about wellness and how to stay healthy on your own, without even going to the doctor.

(Phone hangs up.)

INTERIOR — BAR

Evening. After work at a small, ratty bar. CASSIUS, SALVADOR, *and* MIKE *are sitting in a booth, drinking. They've got their telemarketing scripts on the table.*

CASSIUS: I feel, like, incompetent and an asshole doing this job.

SALVADOR: Funny, I don't feel any different than usual.

(They see a MAN IN A LEATHER JACKET *talking to a* BOUNCER, *who is sitting in front of a door at the back of the bar.)*

SALVADOR: Ay! Ain't that the dude from that show?

MIKE: Oh, hell yeah! That's him! I hate that show.

(The BOUNCER *opens the door and the* MAN IN A LEATHER JACKET *goes through it.)*

CASSIUS: What's that room? I never noticed it before.

MIKE: That's the VIP room.

(A YOUNG COUPLE, *dressed very well, talks to the* BOUNCER *and goes through the door.)*

CASSIUS: What? What the hell is this place doing with a VIP room?

SALVADOR: Don't knock it till you try it. I used to kick it in there all the time. I played it out, though. I'd rather hang out here with the common people.

CASSIUS: What qualifies you to be VIP?

SALVADOR: You need the password. This week it's "upscale elegance." Well, it's always "upscale elegance."

CASSIUS: I'm goin'.

(*SALVADOR and* MIKE *continue drinking and talking while* CASSIUS *walks over to the* BOUNCER, *says the password, and enters.*)

INTERIOR — VIP ROOM

This is a tiny, ten-by-ten-foot room with leather bench seats around the perimeter and a very small, tiled dance floor in the center. At most, four people could fit on this dance floor. The back wall has a service chute—like a small dumbwaiter—above the bench seat. The chute door is closed. There are neon lights on all the walls and flashing disco lights on the ceiling. The music is very loud in the VIP room. The MAN IN A LEATHER JACKET, *the* YOUNG COUPLE *we saw earlier, a* GUY IN A TRACK SUIT, *and two other* WOMEN HOLDING DRINKS *are seated, bobbing their heads to the music.* CASSIUS, *still holding his drink, squeezes into the empty seat between the* GUY IN A TRACK SUIT *and the two* WOMEN HOLDING DRINKS, *bobbing his head as well. It is very crowded. The service chute opens and a very colorful cocktail with an umbrella appears, along with some change. The* MAN IN A LEATHER JACKET *grabs the drink, dancing and leaning over* CASSIUS*—forcing him to quickly turn to the side to avoid having the man's crotch in his face. As Cassius turns, he makes eye contact with one of the two* WOMEN HOLDING DRINKS. *She subtly laughs at him, and he makes an overly cool and flirty face. Just then, the* GUY IN A TRACK SUIT *stretches out, laying his arm over the top of the bench seat as he talks to the* YOUNG COUPLE. CASSIUS *is uncomfortable with this, but instead of saying something he leans toward the two* WOMEN HOLDING DRINKS *to make some space. Four more people come in, one sitting near* CASSIUS *and making him even more uncomfortable. The other three begin to dance. It is crazy crowded in here.* CASSIUS *sips on his drink while still looking at the woman next to him and trying to appear cool, but the ass of an unidentified dancer bumps his drink, spilling it all over his face and shirt.* CASSIUS *politely gets up and leaves.*

INTERIOR — BAR

CASSIUS walks back to the booth where SALVADOR and MIKE are still drinking and sits down. CASSIUS's shirt is wet from the spill.

CASSIUS: (*Nodding*) That was some player shit up in there.

INTERIOR — TELEMARKETING CUBICLES

CASSIUS comes in to start a new workday, script in hand. He sits at a cubicle next to an older black man.

LANGSTON: Hey, youngblood.

CASSIUS: Ay, w'sup.

LANGSTON: Lemme give you a tip. Use your white voice.

CASSIUS: My white voice?

LANGSTON: Yeah.

CASSIUS: But I don't have a white voice.

LANGSTON: Come on, youngblood. You know what I mean. You have a white voice somewhere in there that you can use. Like the voice you use when you get pulled over by the police.

CASSIUS: I use my same voice. For real. (*Jokingly*) I be like, "Back the fuck up off the car and nobody gets hurt!"

LANGSTON: Aight. I'm tryna give you some game. You wanna make money here? Read the script with a white voice.

CASSIUS: Okay. People say I talk white anyway, though, so why isn't it working?

LANGSTON: Well, you don't talk white enough. I'm not talkin' 'bout Will Smith white—that's not even white, that's just proper. I'm talkin' the real deal. Like Al Roker or somethin'. Try it.

CASSIUS: (*Sounding very nasal, pinching his nose*) Hello, Mr. Kramer. I'm Cassius Green. Sorry to bother you—

LANGSTON: No. You got it wrong. It's not about sounding all nasal. It's about sounding like you don't have a care. Like your bills are paid and you're happy about your future and you're about to jump in your Ferrari when you get off this call. Put some extra breath in there. Breezy, like you don't need this money, like you never been fired, only laid off. It's not what all white people sound like—there ain't no real white voice, but it's what they wish they sounded like. It's what they think they're supposed to sound like. Like this, youngblood. (*Overdubbed by a white actor*) Hey! Mr. Kramer! This is Langston from Regalview. I didn't catch you at a bad time, did I?

INTERIOR — MEETING ROOM

We see a crowded meeting room with dry-erase boards on the walls. All the callers are sitting in folding chairs. Three managers stand in front of the room. They are ANDERSON, JOHNNY, *and a woman named* DIANA.

JOHNNY: We all know sales are low, but let's look at why. If you look at the graph, you can see the disgusting lack of contacts reached. People, hit your contacts! You're talking to these assholes for too long. Move the fuck on to the next call. If you're ever gonna be a Power Caller, you gotta know when to bag 'em and when to tag 'em.

(SALVADOR *raises his hand.*)

SALVADOR: Uh, what's bagging and what's tagging?

JOHNNY: Okay. Good question. Bagging is when you drop the call. Like a dead body into a bag, you know? You drop that shit, 'cause it crossed the line. Tagging is when you claim that money. It's a sale. Ch-ching! You tag it. You claim it, like when they put the tag on the body at the morgue to identify it. Sometimes you might bag a dead body and be about to walk away from it and get out of town to lay low and then, instead, you just drag that heavy fucker on into the alley and *then* you tag it. That's when you're really good.

(All of the callers and managers are silent and look very confused.)

ANDERSON: Um, Johnny, those are not authorized catchphrases for this meeting. Everybody, forget that last metaphor, it'll just confuse you. Okay! Diana?

DIANA: Hi, everyone! I'm new here, so forgive me if I don't know all of your names.

(DIANA writes her name on the dry-erase board. It reads DIANA DEBAUCHERY.)

DIANA: My name is Diana Dee-bo-sher-ree.

UNIDENTIFIED CALLER #1: Looks like *debauchery* to me.

DIANA: It's not.

ANDERSON: It's frigid. I mean, French.

(DIANA cuts a mean glare at ANDERSON.)

DIANA: (*Extremely cheerful and too loud*) Anywho! Just call me Ms. D! I'm one of your new Team Leaders! Right now you're probably asking yourself, "Team Leader!? What's a Team Leader? I thought for sure she was a manager and I was a worker! I could've sworn they thought of me as nothing but a collection of motorized appendages that must be coaxed and programmed to do whatever makes the company the most money!"

(Blank stares.)

DIANA: Wrong, my friends! You are not employees anymore, you are Team Members!

CASSIUS: Do we get paid more?

(DIANA smiles while shaking her head "no.")

UNIDENTIFIED CALLER# 2: Anderson is above you guys, right? So then what does that make him, if you and Johnny are Team Leaders?

ANDERSON: Team Manager?

DIANA: No. We're staying away from the word *manager*.

JOHNNY: Coach.

DIANA: Yes, Coach!

ANDERSON: All right, Team Members, that's all for today. Let's get back to work.

JOHNNY: Remember! Hit your contacts! Up the ante! Work the grid! And . . .

(JOHNNY points to an S.T.T.S sign.)

EVERYONE AT MEETING: (*Unenthusiastically*) Stick to the script.

JOHNNY: That's right, Stuss. Any one of you can become a Power Caller and be rollin' in dough!

INTERIOR — TELEMARKETING CUBICLES

SQUEEZE: Ay, man. Seen you around for a couple weeks. We haven't been introduced. They call me Squeeze.

CASSIUS: I'm Cassius. Call me Cash.

SQUEEZE: Good question in there.

CASSIUS: Oh, about getting paid? I was just wondering, 'cause they act like we're supposed to be so hyped about this bullshit.

SQUEEZE: Yeah, right? Well, you cut to the chase, man. (*Very quietly, as if telling a secret*) A player needs to mob up with us for some scrill and bennies.

(*CASSIUS doesn't get it.*)

SQUEEZE: A bunch of us are organizing to make them pay us more and get some benefits. We could use some energy like yours to jump this off—

CASSIUS: Well, I'm real busy with my—

(*SQUEEZE sees JOHNNY looking at him suspiciously.*)

SQUEEZE: We can't talk now. Let's have a drink later. On me.

EXTERIOR — STREET CORNER

DETROIT *twirls a big, arrow-shaped sign that says* OFF! *She twirls it carelessly, occasionally hitting pedestrians and cars.* CASSIUS's *car, loud and backfiring, pulls up and honks. She gets in, sticking her hand out the window to hold the sign outside the car. It's too big to fit. Also in the car are* SALVADOR, SQUEEZE, *and* MIKE. CASSIUS *and* DETROIT *greet each other with a kiss.*

CASSIUS: Off?

DETROIT: Yeah. Off. As in "twenty percent off." (*Smiles*) As in, "My man didn't get me off this morning."

CASSIUS: Stupid.

DETROIT: Who's this?

CASSIUS: Detroit, meet Squeeze, meet Mike. We all work at Regalview together. And you know Gangsta Sal there.

SQUEEZE: Detroit?

DETROIT: My parents wanted me to have an American name.

SQUEEZE: Nice!

CASSIUS: Detroit is a brilliant visual and performance artist—

DETROIT: And no, my art is not twirling signs—

CASSIUS: —who's about to open her first gallery show.

SQUEEZE: Yeah?

DETROIT: And Cassius is my brilliant man who—

(DETROIT *pauses for a second*)

CASSIUS: Exactly. I'm just here, y'all. How would you know I'm brilliant? I don't really do anything.

DETROIT: That's silly, you were—

CASSIUS: You always bring up high school. But look at our high school football team. No, literally. Look at them.

CASSIUS points out the window.

(We see the football team from earlier, scrimmaging in a park.)

CASSIUS: They were stars in high school, now all they do is work at Home Depot and play football every chance they get so they can relive their glory.

MIKE: What's wrong with that? They enjoy it. They're friends.

DETROIT: Baby, can we please not talk about the sun exploding tonight?

(They pass the WorryFree billboard from earlier, the one with the bunk bed and the guy giving a thumbs-up. It has been altered with spray paint, stencil, and wheat-pasted paper. The people in the beds are now wrapped in chains. There is a yellow-triangle caution sign, and the caption now reads: WORRY. SLAVERY AT WORK. It's signed LEFT EYE.)

CASSIUS: I've got bigger ambitions. I don't know what they are, but I'm gonna be something. Part of something.

SALVADOR: Man, you're a telemarketer now, like me. That's something.

(It starts to rain as they drive.)

CASSIUS: D, wiper duty, please.

(DETROIT picks up two strings—tied separately to each wiper—and starts to pull rhythmically left and right, manually making the wipers work.)

SALVADOR: I never get wiper duty!

DETROIT: You can wipe my ass, Sal.

SALVADOR: With my tongue?

CASSIUS: Why not? Your breath already smells like shit.

(The car putters, backfires, and goes dead. White smoke wafts from under the hood.)

SALVADOR: This is a damn bucket!

EXTERIOR — BAR

The whole gang is pushing the car while DETROIT *steers. It's still smoking a little.*

CASSIUS: *(From behind car to* DETROIT*)* Okay! Stop! Stop!

(The car stops in front of a bar. Next to the bar, on the street, are three RVs and a van. Laundry lines hang between the vehicles. Obviously people live in these.)

CASSIUS: It'll start back up after it cools down some more.

SQUEEZE: All right. Drinks on me, everybody.

SALVADOR: *(Singing the E-40 song)* Let's drink! / Get drunk! / Throw up and then! / Get high! / Loaded! / Throw up again!

INTERIOR — BAR

The TV in the bar shows a newscast reporting a violent protest with tear gas, protesters scaling fences, explosions, and police crouching in the middle of the street for cover. Many of the protesters are wearing a single black grease-paint stripe under their left eye.

REPORTER: (*Voiceover*) Today marks the fourth day of violent protests at the WorryFree headquarters in New York City. Protesters claim that WorryFree's lifetime labor contracts constitute a new form of slavery, while WorryFree's spokesperson says that its practices represent a new business model that will save the economy. WorryFree points out that none of its workforce sign contracts under threat of physical violence, so the comparison to slavery is inaccurate.

PROTESTER: (*To reporter*) There is no employment for most people. Even sweatshops have been replaced by WorryFree LiveWork centers. These are prisons. People are packed in like sardines, fed cheap slop, and worked to the bone fourteen hours a day.

REPORTER: Pete, many of the violent protesters are part of the "Left Eye Faction," identifiable by the grease mark under their left eye.

(*The bartender changes the channel. On the TV screen, we see a game show with a large chyron that reads I GOT THE S#*@ KICKED OUTTA ME! The game-show audience is screaming these words out loud.*)

GAME-SHOW AUDIENCE: I got the {beep} kicked outta me!

(*We see a montage of contestants getting beaten with paddles, swimming in a trough of greenish-brown sludge, being pelted with baseballs via a pitching machine—all with a laugh track in the background. The contestants seem afraid or in a lot of pain.*)

BARTENDER: All right, folks! It's Tuesday Boozeday! Half off all drinks!

(*Whoops and whistles throughout the bar.*)

MIKE: I'm just sayin', if you don't cook the spaghetti in the sauce with the cheese in it first: that's some white shit.

CASSIUS: That's some bullshit. How you gon' say what's black and what's white?

MIKE: Well, that's how black folks do it.

CASSIUS: You're wrong. I'm black—

MIKE: You're light black—

CASSIUS: No, I'm *black*. And I cook my spaghetti and then I add the sauce and then I sprinkle some Parmesan cheese on it. Fuck it. Spaghetti is white anyway. It's from Italy.

SALVADOR: Hell no! Italians ain't white!

CASSIUS, DETROIT, AND MIKE: Yes they are!

SALVADOR: Since when!?

SQUEEZE: Since about the last sixty years.

MIKE: Spaghetti is Chinese.

CASSIUS: Speaking of white, I'd like to make a toast.

(CASSIUS clears his throat.)

CASSIUS: (*Overdubbed by a white actor*) To my esteemed Regalview associates whom I revere with great fervor, and to my alluring and phenomenally talented fiancée, I'd like to dedicate this imbibing of intoxicating elixirs. Here's to becoming a Power Caller!

SALVADOR: What the fuck? That's crazy!

MIKE: Oh, shit!

SQUEEZE: Damn!

DETROIT: How the hell did you do that?

CASSIUS: Older dude at the jobby-job showed me. It's the white voice. I guess I'm a natural at it.

SALVADOR: That's some freaky voodoo shit, man. Some supernatural shit.

(CASSIUS shrugs.)

SQUEEZE: The voice thing is crazy, but that Power Caller shit that they feed you is total bullshit. They're trying to hoodwink us.

CASSIUS: Oh yeah?

SQUEEZE: "If you work hard enough as the fry cook, one day you could be the manager! If you twirl that little sign well enough, one day you could twirl a bigger sign at a more glamorous corner!" There might not even be any real Power Callers.

CASSIUS: I saw a dude—

DETROIT: I already have the best corner. And the biggest sign. And the best word. *Off.* It's the anchor to the slogan.

CASSIUS: It sounds like you want me to settle for a life where all I do is work, drink, fuck, and sleep. I wanna matter.

SQUEEZE: You matter more if you're part of something—helping lead something—that changes the world around you.

SALVADOR: I heard they get to sit on silk couches and get blowjobs while they make their calls.

DETROIT: What about the female Power Callers?

SALVADOR: They get blowjobs, too.

SQUEEZE: Look, even if there are Power Callers, if you get a bigger sign, if you become the fry manager: you ain't gettin' much anyway. And what do the rest of us get? Shat on, that's what. We need a union at Regalview. We have to look out for each other and say fuck those fucking fuckers. That way we all get paid.

CASSIUS: *(Overdubbed by a white actor)* Okay. Okay. Well said, brougham. I'm down. *(In his own voice)* Now we all need another half-price drink!

EXTERIOR — CASSIUS'S STUDIO APARTMENT

DETROIT and CASSIUS are rushing out the door. SERGIO is there. He looks sullen.

SERGIO: Hey, Cassius—

CASSIUS: I get paid Friday. I'll have half the money for you then.

SERGIO: Even if you have all the money, that little four months' rent ain't gonna help me. I owe too much. I got word that if I don't have a boatload of money by next month—which I won't—the bank is taking this shit. You should look for a new place.

CASSIUS: Damn.

SERGIO: Making my diabetes act up.

(SERGIO pulls at the feet of the Jesus figure on his gold cross. A pill pops out of the bottom of the cross into SERGIO's hand. We realize that the cross is also a Pez-like pill dispenser.)

CASSIUS: What are you gonna do?

(*SERGIO pops the pill into his mouth and swallows it.*)

SERGIO: I've been talkin' to them WorryFree people. They sent me the brochure. It don't sound that bad. Three hots and a cot, like we used to say.

CASSIUS: Naw. C'mon, Serge. Please don't do that. We can figure somethin' out.

INTERIOR — TELEMARKETING CUBICLES

CASSIUS sits in front of the computer with his headset on. LANGSTON is seated in the cubicle across from him. MIKE is at a cubicle next to him.

CASSIUS: (*Overdubbed by a white actor*) No, thank *you*, Mr. Cyril! If it wasn't for talking to delightful customers such as yourself, well, to be honest, I'd just lose my faith in humanity . . . Now, was that Visa or MasterCard?

(*CASSIUS types as he glances over at the photocopied picture.*)

CASSIUS: Okay! Again, thank you so much. (*To LANGSTON, in his own voice*) Ay, man, this voice thing is workin'!

(*JOHNNY walks up behind CASSIUS.*)

JOHNNY: You are doing so fucking good right now with the voice thing and all, man. But hit those contacts. You've been scoring some big ring-ups in the past few days, but—

CASSIUS: Bagging and tagging.

JOHNNY: Actually, you've just been tagging. Ring-ups are tagging.

CASSIUS: Oh. There's a lot of new lingo—

JOHNNY: All good. Check it. You'll make more money for you and us if you do more calls per hour. You might make less per call, but you'll make more money at the end of the day.

CASSIUS: Okay.

JOHNNY: (*Very quietly*) Oh, and they've been talkin' about you, bro. You are on your way.

(*JOHNNY points up toward the ceiling.*)

CASSIUS: (*Very quietly and earnestly*) To heaven?

JOHNNY: (*Even more quietly*) Almost. PC, baby. Power Caller.

(*CASSIUS smiles and turns back toward the computer to call.*)

MIKE: Told me the same thing three months ago—hey, nice earrings!

(*CASSIUS moves to reveal that the earrings are on DETROIT—now working at Regalview—behind CASSIUS. They are bejeweled erect penises with bejeweled testicles.*)

DETROIT: Thank you. I made them myself.

INTERIOR OF BAR

There's a party going on at the bar. A lot of telemarketers are there. There is a DJ playing music and people dancing. The TV is silently playing I Got the S#*@ Kicked Outta Me! *CASSIUS is sitting at the bar with LANGSTON next to him as SQUEEZE walks up.*

BARTENDER: All right, folks! It's What-the-Fuck Wednesday! Half off all drinks!

CASSIUS: Long Island Iced Tea, neat, please. (*To LANGSTON*) Is it really ever half off if it's always half off?

SQUEEZE: (*Motioning toward the screen*) What kind of world is it when this show is the most popular show in America? They say a hundred and fifty million people watch this every night.

LANGSTON: Personally, I love to see a muthafucka get beat down and humiliated. Makes me feel all warm inside. I got the T-shirt.

(*LANGSTON points to his* I Got The S#*@ Kicked Outta Me! *T-shirt.*)

SQUEEZE: (*To CASSIUS*) Ay, cool if I put my stuff here? I'm gonna go dance, man.

CASSIUS: No problem.

SQUEEZE: In case I don't see you later, you remember to be there early tomorrow, right?

CASSIUS: Fa sho.

(*CASSIUS looks down at what SQUEEZE has set on the stool. A jacket and a newspaper. The newspaper headline reads: SENATE COMMITTEE CLEARS WORRYFREE OF SLAVERY CHARGES. LANGSTON signals the bartender for another drink. The bartender reaches for one of two identical oversize bottles of Jack Daniel's whiskey.*)

LANGSTON: Nuh-uh, man. I want the good shit.

(*The bartender reaches for the other Jack Daniel's bottle. He opens the facade of the bottle—as if it were a door—and we realize that this is a bottle-shaped compartment holding a much smaller bottle. The inner walls of the compartment are wood-grained, and there is a light illuminating the smaller bottle. The bartender grabs the smaller bottle and pours a neat glass for LANGSTON. CASSIUS watches all of this curiously.*)

CASSIUS: (*To* LANGSTON) You ain't dancin', man?

LANGSTON: Hell naw. I'm too old for that shit. Whatever happened to just doin' The Dog? What happened to freakin'? Now you gotta do all this Superman and Spiderman shit. Fuck I look like?

CASSIUS: You crazy, dude. Ay, so is that Power Caller thing for real?

LANGSTON: You've seen them goin' up that elevator, right? Of course it's real.

CASSIUS: But they're supposed to make shitloads of money. Like Benz and big-ass-house-payment money. How the fuck can a telemarketer make money like that?

LANGSTON: If you sellin' the bullshit we're sellin', it's impossible. But they're not sellin' the bullshit we're sellin'.

CASSIUS: Yeah, I guess comparing our job to theirs is like apples and oranges.

LANGSTON: More like apples and the Holocaust.

EXTERIOR — BAR

(*SALVADOR, MIKE, SQUEEZE, and other bar patrons are outside smoking weed and talking excitedly. The football players that they saw the other day are there, too. We hear whoops and hollers. They are all watching a "sideshow," an event in which young people in cars play their music loudly, do doughnuts and "gas-brake dips" {a series of brakes and accelerations that make the car look like a bucking bronco}, and "ghost-ride the whip" {which involves the driver getting out of the car while it is still moving, and walking or dancing beside it}. This is a common occurrence in Oakland, California. CASSIUS approaches SALVADOR, MIKE, and SQUEEZE, who are standing in a circle, smoking. DETROIT walks up to CASSIUS by surprise and hugs him.*)

CASSIUS: Hey, baby!

DETROIT: Hey, lovely. I was hoping to see you earlier. Thought maybe you'd pop up.

CASSIUS: What? At the gallery? You said not to come 'cause all your artist friends were helping you. Didn't you say that?

DETROIT: Yeah, baby. I said that. But that's not what I wanted. I wanted you to be part of it. Don't listen to what I say, listen to what I want.

CASSIUS: I'm confused.

DETROIT: Yes, you are, babylove. But we'll be hanging pieces for a few days. You can pick me up and take me to the gallery on Friday, right?

CASSIUS: Of course, baby. Is cash green?

DETROIT: Yes. Cash is green, Cassius Green.

SQUEEZE: Hey, Detroit. Nice earrings.

(DETROIT *has changed earrings. They are now gold metallic figurines of a hooded man strapped to an electric chair.*)

DETROIT: Thank you, Squeeze.

CASSIUS: Wait—did you change earrings?

(*The camera focus changes away from one of* DETROIT's *earrings to reveal a large billboard across the street behind her. The billboard shows a picture of a black man sitting on a couch with a remote control. He is in exactly the same position as the figurine of the hooded man in the electric chair. The caption under the picture, in big block letters, reads:* SHOW THE WORLD THAT YOU ARE A RESPONSIBLE BABYDADDY. SIGN YOUR FAMILY UP FOR WORRYFREE NOW!)

EXTERIOR — STREET

It's morning. CASSIUS *and* DETROIT *are in the car, puttering their way to work. He drives past the billboard from the night before. It has been altered by street artists. The man on the couch has been changed to a Huey Newton–like figure, holding guns and wearing a black beret. The caption has been altered in a very obvious way—using spray paint and white paint. It now reads:* SHOW THE WORLD YOUR RESPONSE, BABY. FREEDOM NOW! *It is signed* LEFT EYE. DETROIT *looks up at the billboard and smiles.* CASSIUS *notices spray-paint cans on the floor of the passenger side of the car.*

CASSIUS: Tight! You're using spray paint on your new pieces?

DETROIT: Huh? How did you—

CASSIUS: There's paint cans from when you borrowed the car last night to go back to the gallery.

DETROIT: (*Dishonestly*) Yep. Adding some hip-hop to the show.

(As they drive, we see that many people are living in their cars, vans, and RVs. We see a man in an inexpensive suit brushing his teeth in his car, which he is obviously living in.)

EXTERIOR — SIDE OF OFFICE BUILDING

Morning. A group of about thirty people is gathered on the street around the corner from Regalview. They are intently listening to SQUEEZE, *who is speaking loudly in the center of the crowd.* CASSIUS *and* DETROIT *walk up and work their way into the center. Next to the crowd, against the building, there are four makeshift, three-foot-tall shelters with homeless people in them.*

SQUEEZE: . . . and today is gonna be the warning shot that tells them that we stand united. That our demands are serious. A twenty-minute work stoppage during prime calling time. I'm gonna give the call. Mike, what's the call?

MIKE: Phones down!

SQUEEZE: Phones down. Then we all hang up, put down our headsets, and turn off the computers. They're probably gonna single some of us out and threaten our jobs.

LANGSTON: Fuck that.

SQUEEZE: Yes. Fuck that. We ride for anybody they try to fire. Remember why we fight: *we* are making the profits and *they* aren't sharing. I don't know about you, but I want money for rent and food, and I want to be able to go to the doctor when I'm sick. Human decency, man. Now, is anybody not down? Speak now.

DETROIT: (*Startlingly loud and excited*) Fuck that, Squeeze! We ready to roll on these muthafuckas!

SALVADOR: Hell yeah.

CASSIUS: Let's do this. One for all, all for one.

MIKE: That's right. Like the Three Hundred Musketeers.

SQUEEZE: All right, folks. Be ready circa two o'clock.

(*The crowd walks toward the entrance, with* CASSIUS *trailing near the back and* DETROIT *lost in the crowd talking to* SQUEEZE *and* SALVADOR.)

INTERIOR — OFFICE BUILDING LOBBY

As he walks into the building, CASSIUS *sees a couple of men in fancy suits going into the luxurious elevator from earlier. They are accompanied by a couple of stereotypical white female fashion-model types. They are all happily chatting. One of the men turns toward* CASSIUS *and cheerfully winks.*

FANCY SUIT GUY: Don't hurt yourself now.

*(*CASSIUS *stares for a second as the elevator doors close, then keeps walking.)*

INTERIOR — TELEMARKETING CUBICLES

CASSIUS: (*Voice overdubbed by white actor*) Thanks, Mr. Goldberg. As always, we'll be getting that out to you right away. By the way, how is your son's team coming along? I know the little guy was headed for the playoffs . . .

*(*SQUEEZE *stands up and all of the callers go silent.)*

SQUEEZE: Regalview management, you are hereby warned! We will not be overlooked!

MR. GOLDBERG: (*Offscreen*) Hello . . . Hello?

*(*SQUEEZE *takes off his headset as* JOHNNY, ANDERSON, *and* DIANA *watch, bewildered.)*

SQUEEZE: Phones down!

(All of the callers take off their headsets. During the commotion, CASSIUS *looks at* DETROIT *and they smile at each other. Then he looks at the photocopied picture. The man in the picture has a raised fist.* CASSIUS *smiles. He looks again and the photo is back to normal.)*

ANDERSON, DIANA, and JOHNNY are sitting in the office while CASSIUS stands.

CASSIUS: I know you're gonna threaten to fire me. Whatever. If you do, we—

(JOHNNY, DIANA, and ANDERSON laugh.)

JOHNNY: Pack your shit up and get out.

CASSIUS: Fuck you, Johnny. Fuck you, too. Once everybody finds out—

(JOHNNY, DIANA, and ANDERSON laugh.)

ANDERSON: *(Laughing)* What? No, no, no, Mr. Green! You sound a little paranoid! We are the bearers of good news. Great news—

JOHNNY: Great motherfucking news.

ANDERSON: Yes. Great motherfucking news, Power Caller.

CASSIUS: Wait—

ANDERSON: Got the call just now. They think you're Class A material. You're going upstairs, my compadre. You've been promoted. 9 A.M. Tomorrow morning. You have a suit?

DIANA: Of course he does. Strong, powerful, young Power Caller like him.

CASSIUS: Yeah, but . . . okay.

JOHNNY: The big money. The top fucking tier of telemarketing. Making history with legends like Hal Jameson. Badass. How do you feel?

CASSIUS: Um . . . good?

(We hear a pop *and see that* DIANA *has popped a bottle of champagne.)*

CASSIUS: Thanks, Ms. D.

INTERIOR — OFFICE BUILDING LOBBY

CASSIUS *walks through the Regalview doors wearing a very, very fancy bright green suit with a pink tie. He is carrying a briefcase. He walks toward the closed elevator doors.* DIANA *is standing there waiting for him.*

DIANA: Oh. My. You are ready, aren't you?

CASSIUS: Hey, Ms. D. Yeah, I—

DIANA: *(Gesturing toward suit)* Mr. Green, I presume?

CASSIUS: I didn't think about that.

DIANA: Well, let's do this, mu-tha-fuck-ah.

*(*DIANA *inserts the key and turns it to summon the elevator.)*

DIANA: I always wanted to say that. Let's do this, my little gigolo. Do gigolos really get lonely too?

CASSIUS: I don't get it, Ms. D.

DIANA: Oh, you can get it if you want to. And that's not a pep talk.

(The elevator door opens and they both walk in. As before, the elevator has velvet- and leather-covered walls and a chandelier. Macabre harp music is playing. The doors close and DIANA *starts to enter a long code into a keypad.)*

INTERIOR — FANCY ELEVATOR

DIANA: Pink is a bold choice in tie, I must say. It shows a manly confidence—

CASSIUS: I couldn't find my red tie.

DIANA: Well, whatever works.

(The elevator goes up and we hear a woman's voice on the loudspeaker. It is calm and breathy. Music continues in the background.)

ELEVATOR VOICE: Welcome, Power Caller. Today is your day to dominate the world. You are Regalview's elite brigade. Take your place alongside legends like Hal Jameson. You call the shots.

CASSIUS: *(To DIANA)* It's a little strange—

ELEVATOR VOICE: You are in your sexual prime. The top of the reproductive pile.

CASSIUS: What is this crazy shit? Does it really say this every time—

(The elevator door has opened. There are two men standing on the other side of the door. One of them is FANCY SUIT GUY. They have been waiting for CASSIUS.)

FANCY SUIT GUY: *(Overdubbed by white actor)* Welcome to the Power Calling Suite, Mr. Green. Please use your white voice at all times here.

CASSIUS: *(Overdubbed by white actor)* Oh. I'm sorry! I totally didn't realize.

INTERIOR — POWER CALLING SUITE

FANCY SUIT GUY's assistant motions and they follow her through a decadent, plush space that looks like a mix between a posh hookah lounge, a workspace, and a CNN newsroom. There are silk couches, velvet-covered walls, color-coordinated computers, and large flat-screen TVs showing breaking-news clips. They pass a Power Caller who is getting a manicure as he conducts a sales pitch. Everything seems brighter here than in the rest of the world—similar to Dorothy's entry into Oz. FANCY SUIT GUY talks as they walk.

FANCY SUIT GUY: (*Overdubbed by white actor*) Mr. Green, you have been selected not because you are a great telemarketer, but because you have the potential to be a great telemarketer. Do you know what we sell up here?

CASSIUS: (*Overdubbed by white actor*) Well, I heard—

FANCY SUIT GUY: (*Overdubbed by white actor*) We sell power. Firepower. Man power. When U.S. weapons manufacturers sell arms to other countries, who do you think makes that call at the perfect time, which is during dinner?

FANCY SUIT GUY'S ASSISTANT: We do.

FANCY SUIT GUY: (*Overdubbed by white actor*) Before Israel drops a bomb in Gaza, who drops the bomb-ass sales pitch over the phone?

FANCY SUIT GUY'S ASSISTANT: We do.

FANCY SUIT GUY: (*Overdubbed by white actor*) Firepower.

CASSIUS: (*Overdubbed by white actor*) And man power?

FANCY SUIT GUY: (*Overdubbed by white actor*) You know about WorryFree, right?

FANCY SUIT GUY'S ASSISTANT: Of course he does.

FANCY SUIT GUY: (*Overdubbed by white actor*) They're our biggest client. We help thousands of companies bring in WorryFree workers to improve their efficiency.

CASSIUS: (*Overdubbed by white actor*) You sell their slave labor? To other companies? Over the phone?

FANCY SUIT GUY'S ASSISTANT: (*Sarcastically*) We've got a sharp one here.

INTERIOR — BUS DEPOT

A man with a thick mustache and large sunglasses is walking through an indoor warehouse for off-duty buses. He is wearing mechanic's overalls and a hat, and he is carrying a messenger bag. We watch him walk alongside a bus, glancing around to see that the coast is clear. He pulls out a cardboard stencil that says SLAVES *and sprays red paint over it and onto the side of the bus. He walks to another bus and does the same thing. A second man in mechanic's coveralls walks up behind him.*

SECOND MECHANIC: What the fuck are you doing?

(The spray-painting man bolts off, running for the door.)

SECOND MECHANIC: Dave, stop him!

*(*DAVE, *the security guard, is not near the door but runs after the spray painter. He gets hold of him, but the agile spray painter wiggles loose. As the spray painter runs away, we see that his sunglasses have come off, revealing a black grease-paint stripe under his left eye. He pulls off the mustache as well. It's* DETROIT.*)*

DETROIT: (*Yelling*) Left Eye, bitches!

INTERIOR — POWER CALLING SUITE

CASSIUS, FANCY SUIT GUY, and FANCY SUIT GUY'S ASSISTANT are now standing in front of a flat screen showing a WorryFree documentary, which illustrates what FANCY SUIT GUY has been describing.

FANCY SUIT GUY: (*Overdubbed by white actor*) WorryFree is our most important client—they're what's going to make America great again. It's an
ingenious system: the costs of living and the costs of production are
both reduced by having workers live in spare and efficient company
dwellings. Workers sign a lifetime contract, and this allows them to
rest assured that their living situation will be secure for the rest of their
life. There are educational facilities for their children, as well. These
schools prepare the youth of the community for a productive, useful life
as producers. And because there is no need for wages, per se, WorryFree
can make cars for the price it costs others to make bicycles. Some call
it slavery. I call it adaptation.

CASSIUS: (*Shaking head*) I don't know if I can—

FANCY SUIT GUY'S ASSISTANT: White voice.

CASSIUS: (*Irritated*) I don't know if I can—

FANCY SUIT GUY'S ASSISTANT: Here's the starting salary.

(*FANCY SUIT GUY'S ASSISTANT points to his notepad and shows CASSIUS.*)

CASSIUS: (*Overdubbed by white actor*) It looks like I'm gonna have to buy
some more suits. Is there a script?

FANCY SUIT GUY: (*Overdubbed by white actor*) Yes, but it's more complicated,
so it doesn't feel like a script. You'll memorize our facts and catchphrases
until they're second nature. Then you'll start expanding on that founda-
tion and creating sales pitches of your own.

FANCY SUIT GUY'S ASSISTANT: We call it University.

FANCY SUIT GUY: (*Overdubbed by white actor*) You'll be in University until late tonight. We need you in the mix, pronto. We've got a lot to teach you, Cassius Green.

INTERIOR — POWER CALLING SUITE

Montage of CASSIUS *reading textbooks, watching video presentations on large flat-screen TVs, and sitting in on a seminar with a few other students, taking notes.*

EXTERIOR — STREET CORNER

DETROIT *stands alone at dusk on a street corner, twirling an arrow-shaped sign that reads* SIGNS. *She stops twirling the sign intermittently to point it toward the store she is standing next to, which has a big lit-up sign on it that also reads* SIGNS. *Apparently, they're selling signs.* DETROIT *is looking down the street, hoping that* CASSIUS *will show soon. She is wearing gold metallic block-letter earrings that, on her right side, read* BURY THE RAG *and, on her left side, read* DEEP IN YOUR FACE. *A car pulls up. It's* SQUEEZE. *He rolls down the window and yells out.*

SQUEEZE: (*Jokingly*) Ay, baby! What's your sign?

(SQUEEZE *gets out of the car and walks toward* DETROIT.)

DETROIT: (*Smiling*) Pfft! That'd be funny if I hadn't heard it twenty times today.

SQUEEZE: (*Motioning toward the store*) Any deals?

DETROIT: Yep. Seven signs of the apocalypse for the price of one. What are *you* doing here?

(DETROIT *continues twirling the sign.*)

SQUEEZE: Just headed to a meeting and saw you here—so I decided to harass you.

DETROIT: I'm immune. It blends in with the other background noise of the city. Birds chirping, bus engines, police sirens, comments about my ass.

(*We see* SQUEEZE's *eyes look toward* DETROIT's *ass.*)

DETROIT: That was fucking crazy yesterday! Like a scene out of a movie. You were like Norma Rae.

SQUEEZE: I think we have them scared shitless. We'll win. Can I check that out? (*Referring to the sign*)

(DETROIT *shrugs and hands him the sign.* SQUEEZE *starts twirling it in the air, around his back, doing some amazing dance moves.* DETROIT *slyly checks him out. The display of talent makes her smile from ear to ear. A car honks.*)

MAN IN CAR: (*Offscreen*) You tight!

DETROIT: Bravo. Where'd you learn that?

SQUEEZE: Down in LA. We organized the first sign twirlers' union there a couple years ago.

DETROIT: So that's what you do? You go from place to place, stirring shit up? A professional troublemaker.

(SQUEEZE *continues twirling the sign as they talk.*)

SQUEEZE: The trouble is already there. I help folks fix it.

DETROIT: Ha. Shit Fixer Local 123. I admire that. But you're actually a shit starter, like Melquíades in *One Hundred Years of Solitude*.

SQUEEZE: Gabriel García Márquez? Oh, shit. I love him.

(*DETROIT smiles.*)

DETROIT: Me, too. I try to do the same as you do, but with my art. Expose what's fucked about our existence so that people can change it.

SQUEEZE: Not really the same—

DETROIT: It's pretty much the same.

SQUEEZE: I haven't seen your stuff—

DETROIT: (*Partially flirting*) At this rate, you never will—

SQUEEZE: But art is, at most, a complaint. People have complained for centuries.

DETROIT: We're traveling to freedom and travelers need maps. That's what my art can be. Really good, aesthetically pleasing, hopefully expensive maps. But I do other things, too.

SQUEEZE: Oh?

(*SQUEEZE does a behind-the-back move with the sign. He throws it up in the air, spins around, claps three times, and catches it.*)

SQUEEZE: So, does this work with you and Cassius? You sound like a radical and he's . . . I don't know—

DETROIT: He's my best friend. I moved to New York for a while, trying to get my work out there. But I wasn't creating things that felt real.

SQUEEZE: I know that story. Try to move out and make it, but have to move back home.

DETROIT: No. I realized that this is my New York. I'll make it happen here. So I came back. And my friend became my lover. Cash grounds me. But we're so different. I was always driven to engage. He's just now thinking about that.

SQUEEZE: Well, you seem to be rubbing him off right.

(DETROIT *is not sure whether to be offended.*)

SQUEEZE: I mean, you're rubbing on him the right way.

DETROIT: I do more than rub—

SQUEEZE: You know what I mean. He helped with the work stoppage. Your fire is rubbing off on him . . . I mean, I like your fire. I'm gonna go now. You look done here. Do you need a ride?

DETROIT: Nope, Cash is on his way. Thanks, though.

SQUEEZE: Okay. I'll see you around, I'm sure.

(SQUEEZE *reaches and wipes something from under* DETROIT's *eye. It's the faint residue of black grease paint.* SQUEEZE *and* DETROIT *look at the grease paint, which is now on* SQUEEZE's *thumb.* DETROIT *realizes that her cover is blown.*)

SQUEEZE: Nice work.

(SQUEEZE *gets into his car and drives off.* DETROIT *looks down the street for* CASSIUS's *car while she twirls the sign again. Time passes and the sign store's sign turns off.* DETROIT *sits against the wall, still looking down the street and checking her cell phone. Eventually, she sees a bus and runs to catch it, her sign under her arm. The bus has a WorryFree ad on the side:* WHY SLEEP ON THE STREET? WE GOT YOU. WORRYFREE.)

CASSIUS's car pulls up in front of the gallery where DETROIT and friends are hanging her art. CASSIUS runs into the gallery.

CASSIUS: Fuck. I'm sorry, baby. I—

DETROIT: Baby! Are you okay?

CASSIUS: Yeah, I—

DETROIT: Did you get in an accident?

CASSIUS: No—

DETROIT: Break a limb?

CASSIUS: No.

DETROIT: How about robbed? Or something extra crazy yet believable— so I don't think you flaked on me and left me on the corner for an hour.

CASSIUS: I didn't tell you before 'cause I wasn't sure about it, but, as of today, I'm a Power Caller.

DETROIT: Is that a synonym for asshole?

CASSIUS: No, it's a synonym for getting paid, baby. I had to stay late for orientation. It's some crazy—

DETROIT: So, you can pay me back my eighty dollars soon?

CASSIUS: (*Overdubbed by white actor*) Hell yes, baby. No problem!

DETROIT: Stop that. It's freaky.

CASSIUS: Okay. Do I finally get to see your show now?

(*We see that this is a warehouse gallery with thirty-foot ceilings. The walls have been mounted with twenty colorful twenty-foot-tall sculptures of Africa, made with wood, metal, and found objects. There are slogans referencing music, literature, and political movements intertwined in the sculptures. There are also life-size statues of people standing on the floor, looking at the Africas as if they were art connoisseurs. As CASSIUS and DETROIT look at the pieces, DETROIT lights up a joint.*)

CASSIUS: Wow. They're beautiful. And big.

DETROIT: Africa.

CASSIUS: (*Sarcastically*) Oh. Really? Is that what that is?

DETROIT: I'm just sayin'. They're big because they're Africa. Then I just added the statues from my show last year.

CASSIUS: Well, if nobody comes to the opening, it'll look full. Can I ask a question?

DETROIT: You just did—

CASSIUS: You're not African—

DETROIT: I'm not? I'm not white—

CASSIUS: Okay. Why did you choose Africa for this?

(*As DETROIT answers, she accents her statements with grand hand gestures and tokes on the joint. This makes it hard for CASSIUS, who thinks DETROIT is passing him the joint when she gestures. He tries unsuccessfully to grab it from her, but misses it each time and eventually gives up.*)

DETROIT: We're all African. That's where human life started. I wanted to talk about life in America under capitalism. About exploitation, oppression, and the people fighting for power. For a say in their own lives.

(*CASSIUS zones out, focusing on the joint in* DETROIT's *hand. He nods. He can see her lips moving but he isn't listening.*)

DETROIT: . . . to talk about how beauty, love, and laughter are still able to thrive and flourish under almost any circumstances. I realized . . .

(*CASSIUS is still looking at the joint and not hearing her.*)

DETROIT: . . . I needed to talk about how capitalism started. With the theft of labor from Africans. And with you nodding as if you're listening with an interested look on your face, when really you're zoned out, thinking about something else.

(*CASSIUS nods, pretending to listen.*)

CASSIUS: Mmmhmm. Oh. Oh! No. No, I was listening. For real. I was taking it all in. I'm just a little tired. It's hard to focus. Bear with me. Okay?

DETROIT: All right . . . okay.

CASSIUS: Can I hit that joint? So you're doing a performance piece too? Tell me about it.

DETROIT: No. I'm done talking right now. I want to marinate in this. It's major for me. What I want to happen now is for you to sit down with me, hit this weed, and tell me one of your stories.

(*CASSIUS and* DETROIT *sit down on a futon in the middle of the gallery. She lays her head on his chest. With one hand around* DETROIT, *CASSIUS puffs the joint.*)

CASSIUS: Baby, the statues are fuckin' with me. Statues freak me out. Like they might come to life.

DETROIT: Mmmhmm. Baby, start the story.

CASSIUS: Once upon a time, in an apartment twenty blocks away . . .

(Fade out as DETROIT *goes to sleep.)*

EXTERIOR — SIDE OF OFFICE BUILDING

About fifteen callers are gathered in a circle. SQUEEZE *and* MIKE *are addressing them.* SALVADOR *is also in the crowd.* CASSIUS *walks past in a silver zoot suit, carrying a briefcase.*

SALVADOR: Ay! Where you been, man? What's with the suit?

CASSIUS: I got promoted—

SQUEEZE: What? What does that mean? Are you a manager now?

CASSIUS: Naw, man. I'm a Power Caller. About to be paid.

SQUEEZE: Oh. That's interesting, Cassius. Because that's what we're all trying to do. Get fucking paid. But we had a plan to do it together. Teamwork. Are you on the team?

CASSIUS: Yeah, I guess. But I'm on the bench. The bench where you sit and get your bills paid. You know my uncle is about to lose his house?

SALVADOR: The definition of a sellout. You're a walking cliché.

CASSIUS: I'm not sellin' y'all out. My success is not affectin' what you do. Y'all can keep doin' what you doin' and I'll root from the sidelines—and try not to laugh at that stupid-ass smirk on your face.

(SQUEEZE puffs up his chest and gets up in CASSIUS's face. CASSIUS puffs up his chest as well. They both have scowls on their faces. The crowd gathers around them.)

MIKE: Ay, y'all, we don't need this.

(CASSIUS and SQUEEZE stay in their stances, tempers flaring.)

CASSIUS: You doin' all right?

SALVADOR: Oh, I'm doing great. How are *you* doin'?

CASSIUS: I'm havin' a lovely time. You have a good day now.

SALVADOR: You have a better week!

CASSIUS: I will! And may you find this month fulfilling and gratifying!

SALVADOR: I hope your whole year is spectacular. And that's the mutha-fuckin truth! As a matter of fact, I see success in your future!

SQUEEZE: *(Quietly, to no one in particular)* This has taken a turn that none of us could have foreseen.

VOICE FROM CROWD: Are y'all gonna fight or kiss?

MIKE: Both o' y'all: just walk!

(CASSIUS backs up, turns around, and walks into the office building.)

INTERIOR — FANCY ELEVATOR

CASSIUS walks into the elevator and takes a piece of paper out of his pocket. There is a thirty-digit passcode scribbled on it, which he punches into the keypad.

ELEVATOR VOICE: Greetings, Cassius Green. I hope you did not masturbate today. We need you sharp and ready to go. I detect the pheromones percolating out of your pores. They say to others around you: "I have shown up to work ready to kick some ass. Hold my penis while I piss on your criticisms of me." Mr. Green, I am a computer but I wish I had hands to caress your muscular brain. Today is your day.

(The elevator door starts to open but malfunctions: closing and opening repeatedly. Cassius pushes the OPEN DOOR button.)

ELEVATOR VOICE: You have the power to shape the world to your liking. You can make the world bend over at your whim. You—

(Elevator door opens.)

CASSIUS: What is the—

INTERIOR — POWER CALLING SUITE

CASSIUS: *(Overdubbed by white actor)* —deal with that elevator voice thing?

FANCY SUIT GUY'S ASSISTANT: I trust that you've studied all the materials.

CASSIUS: *(Overdubbed by white actor)* Sure did.

FANCY SUIT GUY'S ASSISTANT: Good. We're taking you on a test run.

CASSIUS: *(Overdubbed by white actor)* Test run?

FANCY SUIT GUY'S ASSISTANT: We are a company whose yearly profit margin has more zeros than a roomful of reality-show contestants competing for a date with Tila Tequila. We're not going to let you speak to our valuable contacts without being run through the gamut. Jill, get the Iso-booth ready.

CASSIUS enters an almost pitch-black area barely bigger than a phone booth. He stands there with no clothes on.

FANCY SUIT GUY'S ASSISTANT: (*Offscreen, via loudspeaker*) All right, Green. We'll start you off easy. You can use your normal voice. What does JASSM stand for?

CASSIUS: JASSM is the Joint Air to Surface Standoff Missile.

FANCY SUIT GUY'S ASSISTANT: And what kind of warhead does this missile carry?

CASSIUS: The JASSM carries a one-thousand-pound warhead. It can be fitted with nuclear, chemical, conventional, or even biological warheads.

FANCY SUIT GUY'S ASSISTANT: Good. How much does it cost?

CASSIUS: The JASSM costs 1.5 mi—

(A piercingly loud buzzer sounds, a red light flashes, and CASSIUS is doused from above by a flood of water.)

CASSIUS: Shit! Fuck! Cold!

FANCY SUIT GUY'S ASSISTANT: Wrong. Well, almost right. Say it like a salesman.

CASSIUS: Uh, the JASSM costs three hundred thousand dollars less than the Tomahawk?

FANCY SUIT GUY'S ASSISTANT: Good. What is the average annual rise in profit for first-year clients of WorryFree as compared to the year before?

(Silence.)

CASSIUS: Please repeat.

FANCY SUIT GUY'S ASSISTANT: What percentage is the average annual rise in profit for first-year clients of WorryFree as compared to the year before?

CASSIUS: Can you please rephrase the qu—

(Loud buzzer, red light flashing, CASSIUS is doused with water.)

INTERIOR — POWER CALLING SUITE

CASSIUS walks through the halls of the Power Calling Suite wearing a towel wrapped around his waist. He is carrying his clothes in one arm and his briefcase in the other.

INTERIOR — CASSIUS'S OFFICE

FANCY SUIT GUY'S ASSISTANT: And here is your office. You've been assigned a WorryFree campaign. Brush up on some of that sixth-chapter stuff, and start calling within the next half hour. It's almost dinnertime in Japan.

CASSIUS: Okay.

(CASSIUS, still in his towel, sits at his desk and unfolds the photocopied picture from the cubicle. The man in the photocopied picture has a skeptical look on his face. CASSIUS starts leafing through a manual. He closes it without reading much and picks up the phone. While dialing he looks at a portfolio of his prospective client.)

WOMAN ON PHONE: Softbank, konichiwa!

CASSIUS: *(Overdubbed by white actor)* Konichiwa! Mr. Masayoshi Son, please. This is Cassius Green from WorryFree. Yes, of course I'll hold.

(CASSIUS *listens to hold music.*)

WOMAN ON PHONE: I'm very sorry, but Mr. Son has gone for the evening.

CASSIUS: (*Overdubbed by white actor*) No problem, I'll call his cell.

(CASSIUS *looks at the portfolio for the number and dials.*)

PERSON ON PHONE: Mushi mushi.

CASSIUS: (*Overdubbed by white actor*) Good evening, Mr. Son. It's Cassius Green from WorryFree here. I'm sorry to bother you at dinnertime, but I wanted to talk to you about who's assembling your cell phones . . . No, I *know* they're getting put together in China. The world knows this. I'm here to give you a better deal. I'll cut your labor costs in half. *We've* got the cheap labor now.

INTERIOR — POWER CALLING SUITE

A bunch of sharply dressed Power Callers, including CASSIUS, *are gathered in the Power Calling Suite's lobby.*

FANCY SUIT GUY: (*Overdubbed by white actor*) Let's toast to Cassius Green, already the MVP of the month! He miraculously just made our client upwards of ten million dollars in one call! On the first day, no less! One for the history books. Cheers.

(*The Power Callers raise their glasses and toast.* CASSIUS *walks over to* FANCY SUIT GUY, *who is all of a sudden otherwise engaged. He walks over to* FANCY SUIT GUY'S ASSISTANT.)

CASSIUS: (*Overdubbed by white actor*) Hey, excuse me—

FANCY SUIT GUY'S ASSISTANT: How can I do you for, amigo?

CASSIUS: (*Overdubbed by white actor*) I know that this is my first day here. However, I have just put through a miracle sale and I'm in a terrible financial bind. I . . . (*Normal voice*) I need a cash advance.

INTERIOR — OFFICE BUILDING LOBBY

CASSIUS struts triumphantly out of the elevator and past the windowed work area of the regular callers, who are doing another phones-down protest. He pushes the door open and magically struts straight into his uncle SERGIO'S dining room.

INTERIOR — SERGIO'S DINING ROOM

SERGIO is sitting at the dinner table with his wife and children. He looks up at CASSIUS, who proudly shoves a check in his face. SERGIO reads the check and is visibly moved with joy. SERGIO gets up and hugs CASSIUS while handing the check to his wife, who is also moved. CASSIUS breaks from SERGIO's hug and struts out the door as the couple continues to celebrate.

EXTERIOR — CASSIUS'S STUDIO APARTMENT

CASSIUS struts over to his car, which is still a damn bucket. He opens the driver's-side door, climbs in, and slams the door.

INTERIOR — CASSIUS'S CAR

CASSIUS's bucket is now a brand-new black Mercedes-Benz sports car. He smirks and drives.

EXTERIOR — STREET CORNER

DETROIT is spinning an arrow-shaped sign that says SALE. *CASSIUS pulls up in the Benz. She looks confused and surprised. She hops in, hanging the sign out the open passenger window. They drive to* CASSIUS's *house.*

INTERIOR — CASSIUS'S STUDIO APARTMENT

CASSIUS and DETROIT *fall into bed, making out passionately. The furniture around them changes—one piece at a time—to visibly more expensive versions of every item. First the TV, then the chairs, then the end tables, then the bed on which they continue to make out, which gets too big for the room. Finally, it is clear that they are actually in a large, chic apartment in a different building altogether.*

INTERIOR — CASSIUS'S CHIC APARTMENT

It's morning. CASSIUS *and* DETROIT *are sleeping in a position similar to the scene before, when they were making out.* CASSIUS *wakes, sits up in bed, and stares out the window at a beautiful view of the city. He grabs the remote and turns on the television. On the screen is the WorryFree prison dormitory we saw earlier. There is an oversize, gaudy chandelier hanging in the middle. The decor is Victorian era: six brass bunks and silk blankets. There is fancy wallpaper. Words flash on the screen:* MTV CRIBS: WORRYFREE EDITION!

MTV ANNOUNCER: Up next on *MTV Cribs: WorryFree Edition*: hole puncher Benjamin Ellman.

(The show does a typical MTV-style cut to a shot of BENJAMIN—*a forty-five-year-old white guy—pointing to his bunk, with his wife under the covers. His wife is giving the camera a fake smile.)*

BENJAMIN ELLMAN: *(Overdubbed by a black actor)* This is where the magic happens, baby!

(CASSIUS changes the channel. A man is getting beaten with a dead fish by a man in lederhosen. It's I Got the S#*@ Kicked Outta Me!*)*

GAME SHOW AUDIENCE: I got the [beep] kicked outta me!

(CASSIUS changes the channel. It's the local news. The news cameras show a militant strike, with chanting, picket signs, tussles with the police, and scabs being hit on the head. The strike is in front of Regalview. There are hundreds, maybe thousands of workers involved.)

TV NEWS REPORTER: Chuck, this was the scene yesterday in day forty of the Regalview telemarketers' strike.

(We see about thirty cops with riot gear and shields crouching, shielding themselves, in the middle of an intersection. They are being pelted by a hailstorm of soda cans and rocks from the crowd of protesters. The scene looks very much like footage from student protests in Korea.)

TV NEWS REPORTER: There are only one thousand Regalview workers on strike, Chuck, but they are joined by other telemarketers, phone operators, and university students from all over the area, multiplying their numbers tremendously.

(We see SQUEEZE making a speech to the crowd. He is talking into a bullhorn and a reporter's microphone at the same time.)

TV NEWS REPORTER: This was the scene yesterday—

SQUEEZE: We are telemarketers! We are used to being hung up on! Blocked! And ignored! But we will not let Regalview block, ignore, or hang up on us!

(CASSIUS changes the channel back to MTV Cribs: WorryFree Edition. *They are in an expansive dining hall in the WorryFree complex. There are tables that seem to stretch as long as three city blocks. BENJAMIN ELLMAN walks into frame.)*

BENJAMIN ELLMAN: (*Overdubbed by a black actor*) After a long day of hearty-ass work, you feel me, we ready to eat! This is where we get our grub on—

(*CASSIUS changes the channel back to* I Got the S#*@ Kicked Outta Me! *A contestant is soaking wet, with bloodshot eyes, excitedly talking to the host.*)

GAME SHOW CONTESTANT: Swimming through a vat of hyena urine is not as bad as it sounds!

(*CASSIUS changes the channel back to the news.*)

SQUEEZE: What do we want!? We want enough money to pay the rent!

CROWD: Yeah!

SQUEEZE: We want enough money to eat something besides Cup o' Noodles every night!

CROWD: Yeah!

SQUEEZE: We want to be able to go to the doctor if we get drunk one night!

CROWD: Yeah!

SQUEEZE: Or hook up with somebody without protection!

CROWD: Yeah!

SQUEEZE: And, as a result, think we might have contracted gonorrhea! Or chlamydia! Or any one of those awful, crazy STDs that you never heard of that they have on Self-Diagnosis.com!

TV NEWS REPORTER: Chuck, although strikers have kept most replacement workers from breaking through, every morning Blackwater security guards forcefully and successfully escort Regalview's elite telemarketers—dubbed Power Callers—into the building.

(We see a group of thirty uniformed men in full riot gear, masks, and shields rushing, full speed, toward the strikers. They are all the size of NFL linebackers. They form a protective perimeter around a group of much smaller, fashionably dressed people. In that group: CASSIUS, FANCY SUIT GUY, FANCY SUIT GUY'S ASSISTANT, and others. We especially recognize CASSIUS due to his very bright-colored suit, which contrasts with the gray suits and black uniforms around him. In one fluid—yet violent—motion, we see the Blackwater guards rush, punch, push, and smash their way through the strike line toward the front door. They manage to get the Power Callers into the building, leaving a mass of bloody, enraged strikers behind them.)

TV NEWS REPORTER: For more on the Regalview str—

(CASSIUS turns the TV off. He looks contemplative. He then notices that DETROIT is awake as well, and has been watching the news with him.)

CASSIUS: *(Overdubbed by white actor)* Hey, baby. Good morning.

DETROIT: No. Please no. Stop that stupid voice, Cassius.

CASSIUS: *(Overdubbed by white actor)* I didn't— *(Normal voice)* I didn't even realize—

DETROIT: That's a problem.

CASSIUS: Sorry . . . How long you been awake?

DETROIT: I'm not awake yet. But I saw your TV debut.

(CASSIUS nods knowingly. The man in the framed sepia-tone picture seems to be bowing his head in shame. CASSIUS looks again and the man is back to his normal pose.)

DETROIT: Cash, baby. I c—

CASSIUS: C'mon, can we not—

DETROIT: I can't watch you do this. You're not who I thought you were. You used to just be a sweet little fuck-up. But now you're just fucked up.

CASSIUS: Oh. I'm fucked up? Fuck y—

DETROIT: Look, I quit Regalview when the strike jumped off because being with you made it awkward, but—you abandoned your friends. Even if those weren't your friends—

CASSIUS: I thought they'd just do a few work stoppages and Regalview would cave. Plus, my particular job is not one of the ones they're—

DETROIT: It was one thing when you took the promotion, but now you're a full-on scab. You're on the wrong side, baby. You're crossing the picket line. We've talked about this. I can't ride with you.

CASSIUS: Oh? You seemed to be ridin' pretty good when I—

DETROIT: No more.

CASSIUS: What are you sayin'? You're askin' me to quit the fattest job I've ever had or that I'm ever gonna—

DETROIT: It's not fat. It's morally emaciated. Starving. Cash. You sell fucking slave labor.

CASSIUS: One of the reasons I took this job—besides the money—was to make myself interesting enough to keep you with me. Now I'm finally somebody important. I make shit happen. You can't see it because you've always had that.

DETROIT: Cash. What? You were worried about losing me? Okay. If you go to work today at Regalview—crossing the strike again, and selling evil—I can't be with you.

EXTERIOR — OFFICE BUILDING

CASSIUS is in the middle of the other Power Callers, who are in the middle of the Blackwater guards. They are across the street from the Regalview building and the strikers.

BLACKWATER AGENT #1: Elbows and assholes, people! Let's go!

OTHER BLACKWATER GUARDS: Hut! Hut! Move!

(They run quickly together. Although we see only CASSIUS's face during this shot, we hear the thuds and curses of strikers and Blackwater guards.)

INTERIOR — POWER CALLING SUITE

CASSIUS and other Power Callers file out of the elevator. CASSIUS slowly walks to his office and sits down. He looks around: business as usual. He opens a portfolio and begins to make a call. He sees FANCY SUIT GUY'S ASSISTANT.

FANCY SUIT GUY'S ASSISTANT: Well, we made it.

CASSIUS: (*Overdubbed by white actor*) We sure did . . . I'm gonna just follow up on this thing I've been working on.

FANCY SUIT GUY'S ASSISTANT: Okey dokey.

(CASSIUS stops, as if having second thoughts. He looks over at the photocopied picture. The man seems to be staring disapprovingly. He looks again and the man in the picture is back to his normal pose. He shakes it off and dials confidently.)

INTERIOR — POWER CALLING SUITE

The Power Callers are all gathered in the Power Calling Suite lobby.

FANCY SUIT GUY: (*Overdubbed by white actor*) This. Mother. Fucker. Is. On. Fire! Let's toast to the boy wonder!

(The Power Callers raise their glasses and toast to CASSIUS, *who looks very proud and accomplished.)*

EXTERIOR — STREET

CASSIUS *drives down the street in his new car. He parks in front of the gallery, where* DETROIT *is hanging up more Africa sculptures with help from a half dozen others. There is a giant poster that says her show will open the following day.* CASSIUS *watches* DETROIT *through the big windows for a few seconds, then speeds off.*

INTERIOR — CASSIUS'S CHIC APARTMENT

CASSIUS *sleeps alone in his big bed.*

EXTERIOR — OFFICE BUILDING

CASSIUS, *again, is surrounded by other Power Callers who are surrounded by Blackwater guards. Once again they all run across the street together, straight toward the strikers. We see the hand of one of the strikers shaking up a Coke can and throwing it. It sails beautifully through the air and lands perfectly on* CASSIUS's *forehead, which gushes with blood.*

CASSIUS: Fuck!!!

FEMALE VOICE: (*Offscreen*) Have a Coke and a smile, bitch!

(The group continues its blitz into the building.)

INTERIOR — POWER CALLING SUITE

FANCY SUIT GUY is standing outside of CASSIUS's office, watching as CASSIUS finishes up a call. CASSIUS notices FANCY SUIT GUY while hanging up. CASSIUS has a bandage on his head.

FANCY SUIT GUY: *(Overdubbed by white actor)* You, my friend, are the best decision I've made in quite a long time. Raw talent. I have to pat myself on the back. No. You're such a boon to our productivity that I should pat myself on the ass.

CASSIUS: *(Overdubbed by white actor)* Well, thank you, Mr. _____. *(Whenever FANCY SUIT GUY's name is said, it is bleeped out and the mouth of the person speaking is pixelated to hide the name.)* It's good to be appreciated.

FANCY SUIT GUY: *(Overdubbed by white actor)* Don't call me Mr. _____. Call me _____. Cassius, do you like to party?

CASSIUS: *(Overdubbed by white actor)* I like parties.

FANCY SUIT GUY: *(Overdubbed by white actor)* What are you doing tonight?

CASSIUS: *(Overdubbed by white actor)* I've got a couple things to follow up on here and my girl—I mean my ex-girl—has a—

(Blood is dripping from CASSIUS's bandage onto his face.)

FANCY SUIT GUY: *(Overdubbed by white actor)* Maybe you should have that looked at.

CASSIUS: *(Overdubbed by white actor)* No, I'm fine.

FANCY SUIT GUY: (*Overdubbed by white actor*) Well, about tonight—I know it sounds like I'm asking, but actually, I'm demanding. You have to come. As you know, Steve Lift is the CEO of WorryFree. He throws a yearly party and it's the kind of party that kings wish they got invited to. Puffy can't even get an invite. Steve Lift wants to speak to our new star. That's you.

CASSIUS: (*Overdubbed by white actor*) I can't. I have to—

FANCY SUIT GUY: (*Overdubbed by white actor*) I won't accept no for an answer. Go to your other thing and I'll pick you up after. It could change your life—

CASSIUS: (*Overdubbed by white actor*) Again?

FANCY SUIT GUY: (*Overdubbed by white actor*) This kind of party . . . this is where the magic happens.

INTERIOR — GALLERY

The gallery is filled with people who are dressed to the nines. This is the opening of DETROIT's *show.* CASSIUS *walks in and makes his way through the crowd toward* DETROIT. *She is at the other end of the room, talking to a circle of art enthusiasts. Once again she is wearing metallic earrings: the right one says* YOU'RE GONNA HAVE TO FIGHT *and the left one says* YOUR OWN DAMN WAR.

DETROIT: (*Overdubbed by an actor with a British accent*) . . . the greed of a few who turn the rest of us and our lives into commodities, which are used to create other commodities. I wanted to talk about how beauty, love, and laughter are able to thrive and flourish under almost any circumstances. I realized that in order to do all that, I needed to talk about how capitalism started. By stealing labor from Africans. And, of course, land from indigenous—(*DETROIT sees* CASSIUS *coming toward her.*) Please excuse me for a moment?

(DETROIT walks over to CASSIUS.)

CASSIUS: I wouldn't miss this for the world. Congratulations. This is beautiful. You're beautiful. I love you—

DETROIT: You know I love you, too. But I can't hang with the craziness. You're cold inside now. I feel it. Something disconnected. What happened to your head?

CASSIUS: Don't worry about it. You should see the other guy.

DETROIT: I have to go get ready for the performance. Are you staying to see it? You really should.

CASSIUS: I can stay for a little, but I have to meet an important person at a party.

DETROIT: Oh, a fellow slave auctioneer?

(CASSIUS grabs an already-poured glass of champagne from the bar right next to them. He looks up and SAL and SQUEEZE are walking toward him.)

DETROIT: Hey, Squeeze. Thank you so much for coming.

SQUEEZE: I wouldn't miss this for the world.

DETROIT: You always know the right thing to say.

CASSIUS: I said that a second ago.

(DETROIT walks away.)

SALVADOR: Man, we were friends. Do you not call me anymore because you're a sellout, or because you're a star?

CASSIUS: A star? What—

(SALVADOR shoves a smartphone in front of CASSIUS's face. There's a YouTube clip paused on a blurry Coca-Cola can in flight over the heads of a crowd. Salvador presses play and the video shows the can hitting CASSIUS's head. It's the scene from that morning. When the can hits, a cartoonlike sound effect can be heard. Salvador laughs loudly and puts the smartphone back in his pocket.)

SALVADOR: Eleven million views already, man! You're the Justin Bieber of backstabbers.

SQUEEZE: Look, man. We could really use your help right now. We have them by the balls financially, but they're holding out. We're at an important point, tactically. We've done the research on how much this is costing them. If we can make them lose just a little more, they'll be willing to meet our demands. You jumping sides now could really turn the tide.

CASSIUS: I—

SQUEEZE: We've never been close and I don't like what you did. But I saw something in you at first and I think it's still in there. Don't be that leaf that goes wherever the river takes you: be the stone that shifts the stream.

SALVADOR: Shit. Piss your own stream, man.

CASSIUS: Squeeze, man. I hear you, but let's talk about it this weekend. I gotta think about it.

SALVADOR: Wha—

SQUEEZE: Okay. I'll call you. For real.

CASSIUS: For real. We'll talk at least.

(A gong sounds and everyone in the gallery turns toward it. DETROIT is standing at the gong, wearing a black trench coat and aviator sunglasses.)

DETROIT: (*Overdubbed by an actor with a British accent*) Welcome, friends! Gather around, but form a semicircle by staying on the other side of those lines. Tonight, we will have a transformative experience. In those containers there are broken cell phones, used bullet casings, and water balloons filled with sheep's blood. Cell phones can only work with the mineral coltan, which is found only in Africa's Congo. The profit involved in this has created hardship and wars. I will stand here, and if you feel so moved, you may throw the items in the containers at me. While I stand here, I will be reciting an excerpt from the timeless Motown-produced movie *The Last Dragon*. I will recite the lines that Angela says to Eddie Arcadian as she leaves him.

(*DETROIT takes the trench coat off and is naked, save for the sunglasses.*)

DETROIT: (*Overdubbed by an actor with a British accent*) Let's begin.

(*DETROIT bangs the gong.*)

DETROIT: (*Almost whispering, overdubbed by an actor with a British accent*) And in the end, Eddie, you know what? You're nothing but a misguided midget asshole with dreams of ruling the world. Yeah, also from Kew Gardens. And also getting by on *my* tits.

(*Silence.*)

DETROIT: (*Softly, overdubbed by an actor with a British accent*) And in the end, Eddie, you know what? You're nothing but a misguided midget asshole with dreams of ruling the world. Yeah, also from Kew Gardens. And also getting by on *my* tits.

(*One cell phone is thrown. Then a bullet casing.*)

DETROIT: (*A little louder, overdubbed by an actor with a British accent*) And in the end, Eddie, you know what? You're nothing but a misguided midget asshole with dreams of ruling the world. Yeah, also from Kew Gardens. And also getting by on *my* tits.

(*Water balloons of blood explode against* DETROIT'*s body. Cell phones and bullets are being thrown. It looks painful.*)

DETROIT: (*Yelling, overdubbed by an actor with a British accent*) And in the end! Eddie! You know what!? You're! Nothing! But a misguided midget! Asshole! With dreams! Of ruling the world! Yeah! Also from Kew Gardens! And also! Getting by on *my* tits!

(DETROIT *is really getting pelted.* CASSIUS *angrily rushes into the middle of the chaos, dodging as he goes.*)

CASSIUS: Ay! Ay!! Stop! Wait a fucking minute! (*The pelting stops.*) Stop! What the hell is going on here?! (*To* DETROIT) Why would you subject yourself to this?

DETROIT: It's part of the show. You, of all people, should know that. Stick to the script.

(DETROIT *reaches down, grabs a black football helmet, and puts it on.*)

DETROIT: Don't you have a party to go to? (*To the audience, overdubbed by an actor with a British accent*) Begin again! And in the end! Eddie! You know what!? You're! Nothing . . .

(CASSIUS *gets out of harm's way, walks through the crowd, and exits the gallery as the soliloquy and pelting continue.*)

INTERIOR — STEVE LIFT'S MANSION

We see a close-up of a nose snorting an extra-long line of cocaine. It takes about ten seconds to finish the line. The nose belongs to STEVE LIFT. *He lifts his head quickly.*

STEVE LIFT: I guess you're all wondering why I've called this meeting!

(*Laughter. A DJ spins a record and loud music starts. About two hundred people are partying in an extremely decadent mansion. Some are talking on couches and chairs. Some are standing. Some are dancing. Most of them are drinking and smoking weed. Ninety-nine percent of them are white.*)

FANCY SUIT GUY: (*Overdubbed by white actor*) Hey! Steve!

STEVE LIFT: Well, helloooooo _____! You motherfucking motherfucker! Are you loving the new digs or what?

(*Subtitle reads: "My dick is bigger than yours, FYI."*)

FANCY SUIT GUY: (*Overdubbed by white actor*) Love it.

(*Subtitle reads: "Yes, boss. Your dick is bigger than mine."*)

STEVE LIFT: Stick around, because most of these bitches are probably gonna get naked later!

(*Subtitle reads: "Again, my dick is bigger than yours and most of these lovely women are actually going to get naked later. For real."*)

FANCY SUIT GUY: (*Overdubbed by white actor*) Of course! Your parties are the stuff of folklore. Steve, meet the man of the hour—

CASSIUS: (*Overdubbed by white actor*) Cassius Green. It's a pleasure to meet you. An honor.

STEVE LIFT: Hola, compadre! Necesitan algun . . . a tuto . . . aw, fuck. Who am I kiddin'? I don't speak Mexican! I don't mean to offend, though. You're not one of them Spanish people that just looks black, are you?

CASSIUS: (*Overdubbed by white actor*) No, Mr. Lift. I'm just black.

STEVE LIFT: Please, don't call me Mister.

CASSIUS: (*Overdubbed by white actor*) Okay. Steve.

STEVE LIFT: Nope. That doesn't feel right. Just call me sir.

CASSIUS: (*Overdubbed by white actor*) Yes, sir—

STEVE LIFT: I'm just foolin'! Call me whatever the fuck you want—just keep makin' that fucking money! Woo! You must be a fucking genius. I'd love to pick your brain, because we need more people like you over at WorryFree. People who can comprehend the bigger picture. It's people like you who are gonna save this nation, Green. I mean, don't get me wrong—we need the workers to do the actual work. But we need people like you, too, who can be trusted. People who can analyze the challenges and adapt . . . like a snake. Or a cockroach. Or a little fiendish raccoon scavenging through a garbage can.

CASSIUS: (*Overdubbed by white actor*) Thanks.

INTERIOR — GALLERY

The gallery is almost empty. There is a gigantic mess on the floor: bullet casings, broken cell phones, and water. There are three people cleaning up: SQUEEZE, DETROIT, and a female friend of DETROIT's, SAMIYAH.

SAMIYAH: This was a really beautiful event.

DETROIT: Thank you! And thank you guys for helping me clean. I think I'm gonna do the rest tomorrow. I'm fucking tired.

SAMIYAH: Cool. I gotta get back to my little ones anyway.

(*SAMIYAH heads for the door.*)

DETROIT: Thank you, Samiyah! I love you!

SAMIYAH: I love you, too!

(*SAMIYAH exits.*)

DETROIT: (*To SQUEEZE*) So, what did you think?

SQUEEZE: It was . . . fiery.

(*DETROIT smiles knowingly and locks the door. Then SQUEEZE and DETROIT make out aggressively while slipping around on the wet floor, bullet casings, and broken cell phones.*)

INTERIOR — STEVE LIFT'S MANSION

The party is still happening. STEVE LIFT, CASSIUS, FANCY SUIT GUY, and a bunch of others are sitting on and around a couch. Some people are still dancing. Those on the couch and around it are listening intently to STEVE LIFT.

STEVE LIFT: . . . I had to climb up on the side of the overturned jeep and pry the AK from under the crushed seat where my dead and bloody guide was. When the rhino charged again, he got a head full of lead. Brrr-rat-ta-ta-ta-ta! Brains all over the place. I made that motherfucker into a trophy.

(*STEVE gestures toward a wall where a disgusting, gory, tattered head of a rhinoceros is mounted.*)

STEVE LIFT: Hey, Cassius. You ever had to put a cap in anybody's ass?

(*Laughter.*)

FANCY SUIT GUY: (*Overdubbed by white actor*) Green? No—

STEVE LIFT: Shut up, _____. I'm talking to the man of the hour here. I wanna hear about some of that Oakland gangsta shit. Oaktown!

CASSIUS: (*Overdubbed by white actor*) No, sir. Luckily, I haven't had to cap anybody yet. Sorry. No gangster stories for ya.

STEVE LIFT: Hmmm, okay. Give us somethin', man! We work hard, we party hard. These type of motherfuckers are at my party every year. You're different. Leave an impression. At least take off the white voice. I know you can at least bust a rap for us or somethin'.

CASSIUS: Actually, I can't rap worth shit. It's embarrassing.

STEVE LIFT: Bullshit!

CASSIUS: For real, I don't rap. I don't know how to rap. I'm hella good at *listenin'* to some rap, though.

STEVE LIFT: Fuck that, man! You're lying! Rap! Rap! Rap! Rap!

(*First* FANCY SUIT GUY *begins to chant, "Rap! Rap! Rap! Rap!" as well, and then the whole party catches on.* CASSIUS *slowly and reluctantly heads toward the DJ booth after being handed a microphone. The crowd is hyped: whooping, hollering, and dancing hard to the instrumental that the DJ is playing.* CASSIUS *bobs to the beat to stall a little. Finally—*

CASSIUS: W'sup . . . My name is Cash / I love to . . .

(*He can't finish.*)

PERSON AT PARTY: Smash!

CASSIUS: One, two . . . I come from the city of dope / Couldn't be saved by John the Pope / I like to . . .

(He can't finish. He goes back to bobbing his head and slightly dancing. The music does a drum fill, and then kicks into the chorus. CASSIUS gets an idea and comes in on the beat, looking unsure.)

CASSIUS: Nigga shit! Nigga, nigga, nigga shit! / Nigga shit! Nigga, nigga, nigga shit! / Nigga shit! Nigga, nigga, nigga shit!

(The crowd reacts wildly and chants along with CASSIUS. Everyone dances, some of them freaking and doing booty dances. Certain people are on the couches, others on chairs and tables. This seems to go on for a while. We see from CASSIUS's facial expression that he is troubled by the whole thing.)

INTERIOR — STEVE LIFT'S MANSION

CASSIUS sits in a chair alone, drinking a glass of bourbon, while the party continues around him. He stares ahead blankly, disconnected from the raucous gathering. He is obviously upset about his performance. His formerly white bandage is partly brownish red with blood. His wound is still bleeding. He wipes his forehead with a handkerchief. FANCY SUIT GUY kneels down beside him. His nose has white powder all over it.

FANCY SUIT GUY: Yo, Steve wants you back there.

(FANCY SUIT GUY is not speaking with his white voice. He has a southern accent, we realize for the first time. He motions toward a closed door at the back of the room.)

FANCY SUIT GUY: Go through that door, all the way down the hall. Make a right, then a left . . . then go through the third door on your left, make a right, and you'll see it. It's the magenta door . . .

(CASSIUS gets up.)

FANCY SUIT GUY: This could be big. Don't fuck it up.

(As CASSIUS walks away, we see that a small group of people is watching a You-Tube video of CASSIUS being hit by the Coke can. They are laughing hysterically.)

INTERIOR — MANSION HALLWAY

CASSIUS opens the first door and goes through it. He walks down a lavishly decorated hallway. Then he turns and is in a different kind of hallway. It's white. It almost looks like a hospital. He turns again and now he's walking down a hallway with windowed rooms on either side. They are laboratories, their lights off for the night. One of the rooms is full of levers, ropes, pulleys, and metal wheels. He finally gets to the door he's looking for, which is painted magenta, and enters.

INTERIOR — LIFT'S PRIVATE OFFICE / LOUNGE

CASSIUS enters a spacious and luxurious room. The principal feature of the room is a massive desk, behind which is a large video screen. The room is decorated with an equine motif: there are paintings—some small, some oversize—of horses and centaurs. One of the pieces, which involves a woman and a horse, is quite sexual. The desk itself is a ridiculously gaudy thing. Its legs are two sculptured horses. There is a small dish of apples on it. STEVE LIFT is behind the desk, leaning back in his chair. He seems coked out and has a small mirror in front of him. It's covered in cocaine and a straw. He throws an apple to CASSIUS, who catches it.

STEVE LIFT: Heads up!

CASSIUS: This room is nuts.

STEVE LIFT: Thank you. I'll accept that as a backhanded compliment. Pull up a chair, Cassius Green.

(CASSIUS sits.)

STEVE LIFT: Is your head okay?

CASSIUS: My ex doesn't think so.

STEVE LIFT: Well, here in Lift's lair, we'll do no line before its time. And it's time, my friend. You're rollin' with the big dogs.

(STEVE LIFT *pushes a commemorative plate from* The Mr. Ed Show *across the table toward* CASSIUS. *On the plate is a line of cocaine that circles around in a spiral shape.* CASSIUS *pauses for a second, then snorts the spiral line.*)

CASSIUS: Shit!

STEVE LIFT: I wanna propose something, Cash.

CASSIUS: And I wanna listen to your proposal, Stevie.

STEVE LIFT: We need you at WorryFree. I see something in you. You're more than just the best telemarketer the world has seen since Hal Jameson.

CASSIUS: That's interesting. Yet boring. Tell me something I don't know. Something with zeros and commas.

STEVE LIFT: Cocky. I like that. You'll understand the proposal if you watch this video we put together.

CASSIUS: Can I take a piss first?

STEVE LIFT: No.

(STEVE LIFT *picks up a remote control and starts the video. It's a commercial video showing still pictures of factories from the late 1800s. Corny electronic music plays as these pictures flash on the screen.* CASSIUS *is watching uncomfortably and obviously has to pee.*)

VIDEO NARRATOR: When the industrial revolution—

CASSIUS: I actually hella have to piss.

(The video pauses.)

STEVE LIFT: Fine. It's the jade-colored door on your right. Hurry back.

INTERIOR — MANSION HALLWAY

CASSIUS rushes out the door into the hallway. He finds the jade door and opens it.

INTERIOR — WASHROOM

The room is darkly lit, with bathroom tiles on the wall, a sink, a mirror, some curtains for what seem like showers, and one metallic stall. The room has a sanitary feel to it. We know there's a guy in the stall because we can see his head.

CASSIUS: Fuck! Only one stall? Are you on your way out or in?

GUY IN STALL: Can you help me?

(CASSIUS walks toward the stall. The man's breathing is audibly heavy.)

CASSIUS: Naw, man. Is this some . . . I'm not—

GUY IN STALL: Please, help me. I'm fucked up. I'm hurting.

(GUY IN STALL leans suddenly against the door and bumps it, as if ready to fall.)

CASSIUS: Aight. Hold on, m—

(CASSIUS opens the stall door, revealing a naked part-man, part-horse. The shape of his body is much closer to a horse's than a human's. There is no hair on his entire man-horse body, except for the normal patches of hair that a semi-hairy man might have. Unlike a mythical centaur, the man has no extra limbs. His hind legs have human feet, his front legs have human hands. He is very sweaty and has humongous horselike nostrils. His human eyes show that he is terrified. He is chained and

collared to the stall. He lets out a chilling whinny. CASSIUS *is suddenly terrified and screams out while backing up.)*

CASSIUS: Fuck! Shit! Fuck, fuck, fuck, fuck, fuck! What the fuck! What the fuck!

GUY IN STALL: Please, help me. I'm hurting.

*(*GUY IN STALL *lets out a whinny.* CASSIUS *turns to run out, but the floor is slippery and he runs into one of the shower curtains, bumping something behind it. This is not actually a shower, but another stall. Another man-horse sticks his head out from behind the curtain. He whinnies.)*

SECOND GUY IN STALL: Please help me. I'm hurting.

(Other horse-men and women stick their heads out of curtains, whinnying, neighing, and saying, "Please help us.")

INTERIOR — MANSION HALLWAY

CASSIUS *bolts out of the door and straight into* STEVE LIFT.

CASSIUS: The fuck!?

STEVE LIFT: Asshole! I said the jade door!

CASSIUS: That *is* the jade door!

STEVE LIFT: That door is obviously olive! Not jade! It is very clearly an olive-colored door!

CASSIUS: Get me the fuck outta here!

*(*STEVE LIFT *places his hand on* CASSIUS'S *shoulder.)*

STEVE LIFT: Okay. Big, big misunderstanding. Let's both calm down. Let's breathe. Let's go back to my office. I'll explain. Do you still have to go pee?

CASSIUS: I pissed in my fucking pants, man. So, no, I don't have to pee anymore. I am so fucking outta here!

(*CASSIUS shakes his shoulder free of* STEVE LIFT *and turns to run away.* STEVE LIFT *pulls a silver 9mm pistol from the small of his back.*)

STEVE LIFT: Okay. Breathe. Calm. Big misunderstanding. Let me explain.

INTERIOR — LIFT'S PRIVATE LOUNGE

CASSIUS sits in his chair while STEVE LIFT *leans back on the desk, facing him. We see that the pistol is still in* STEVE LIFT'S *hand.* CASSIUS *is sweating, nervous, and scared.*

STEVE LIFT: Dude. I can't let you go without explaining. If you had seen the video before you saw everything in there, you wouldn't have gotten scared.

CASSIUS: And just what in the fuck was "everything in there"?

STEVE LIFT: The video will explain.

(*STEVE LIFT clicks the remote. The video plays from where it was paused. It is clear that the factories in the stills were actually miniature models of factories. The stills are now moving, and we realize that we are watching stop-motion animation. The screen shows the WorryFree logo, which quickly fades out. The screen then reads* THE NEW MIRACLE, *and underneath that* DIRECTED BY MICHEL GONDRY.)

STEVE LIFT: (*Offscreen*) We paid a pretty penny for this shit.

(*All the words fade out. Fade in on a lush green countryside with hills and streams, all brought to life by stop-motion animation. A group of six Neanderthal-like apes are trying to break open a coconut. They are banging it on the dirt and pounding it with their hands. One of the Neanderthals, a female, turns and walks toward the camera, naked and very hairy, with hairy breasts and nipples visible.)*

NEANDERTHAL WOMAN: (*In a British accent*) Since the dawn of time—or at least since before anyone cares to remember—we have used our wits to survive.

(A smaller Neanderthal snatches the coconut from a bigger Neanderthal and smashes it against a rock, cracking it open. The Neanderthals cheer with apelike sounds of excitement.)

NEANDERTHAL WOMAN: But what allowed us to *thrive* was our use of tools. A natural development.

(The bigger Neanderthal lets out a shrill, furious scream, and smashes the back of the smaller Neanderthal's head with a big, pointed rock. The smaller Neanderthal falls over dead. The others look on in horror. The animation rewinds and the frame freezes on the bigger Neanderthal's arm as it smashes the rock into the smaller Neanderthal's head. Blood and pieces of skull are spurting out, frozen in mid-air.)

NEANDERTHAL WOMAN: But what are tools . . .

(A red dotted line is superimposed over the bigger Neanderthal's arm, from the shoulder to the tip of his fingers. A caption reads ARM.)

NEANDERTHAL WOMAN: . . . if not extensions of the appendages with which we were born?

(A yellow dotted line is superimposed over the rock that the bigger Neanderthal is holding. It runs from the tip of his fingers to the end of the rock, which is partly inside the smaller Neanderthal's head. A caption reads ROCK. The yellow dotted line turns red and the caption reading ROCK disappears. The ARM caption moves to the

center of the screen. The arm turns into a Homo sapiens arm and the rock turns into a hammer. The arm and hammer are hammering a nail. Then the hammer turns into a TV remote control. The hand clicks the remote.

NEANDERTHAL WOMAN: (*Offscreen*) Humans sometimes need modification to perform better in a specified situation. So we have modified ourselves throughout history.

(We see boxers sparring in a boxing ring as NEANDERTHAL WOMAN walks through the frame.)

NEANDERTHAL WOMAN: We train ourselves to fight.

(NEANDERTHAL WOMAN walks into a weight room.)

NEANDERTHAL WOMAN: We work out.

(NEANDERTHAL WOMAN walks into a dorm room where someone is working at a desk.)

NEANDERTHAL WOMAN: We study. These changes to the body and mind are actually chemical changes.

(The dorm room fades away and the WorryFree logo appears behind NEANDERTHAL WOMAN.)

NEANDERTHAL WOMAN: WorryFree is carrying forward this lineage of natural developments that began in prehistoric times. We are proud to announce to our shareholders that a new day in human productivity is dawning.

(A scientific laboratory appears behind NEANDERTHAL WOMAN, with scientists working.)

NEANDERTHAL WOMAN: Our scientists have discovered a way—a chemical change—to make humans stronger, more obedient, more durable, and, therefore, more efficient and profitable.

(*A factory assembly line appears behind* NEANDERTHAL WOMAN, *with workers pulling levers on machines, lifting widgets from a conveyor belt, etc.*)

NEANDERTHAL WOMAN: At WorryFree, we realize that human labor is more efficient than robot labor when it comes to adaptability of movement. But human labor has its limitations.

(*The workers transform into big, hulking horse people. They are lifting more widgets, pulling bigger levers on bigger machines, producing more widgets. They all have happy looks on their faces.*)

NEANDERTHAL WOMAN: We are breaking those limitations. Our workforce of equisapiens will make WorryFree the most profitable company in human history. And you, our shareholders, will be a part of that history.

(STEVE LIFT *stops the video.*)

STEVE LIFT: See what I'm talkin' about? Big misunderstanding.

CASSIUS: Uhn-uhn. No! What do you mean? There is no fucking misunderstanding. Are those half-horse, half-people that you have created in a lab so you can make more money?

STEVE LIFT: Well, yeah. I just didn't want you to think I was crazy or something. I'm doing this to help turn a profit—it's not irrational.

CASSIUS: Aight. Cool. I understand and I would like to leave now. Please.

STEVE LIFT: But I didn't even get to make my proposal to you.

(*CASSIUS starts to get up.*)

CASSIUS: Can you call me tomorrow about that? I need to leave now, but I'm very interested.

(*STEVE LIFT puts his hand on the gun. CASSIUS sits.*)

STEVE LIFT: You have to see the rest of the video. There's a lot of production value. Then my proposal.

(*STEVE LIFT clicks the remote and plays the video. The animated video shows factory workers lining up in several lines to go through doors.*)

NEANDERTHAL WOMAN: Our worker-modification process is simple and rather quick. It works for 70 percent of humans who take the fusing catalyst.

(*The workers walk through the doors and are handed silver straws by men and women in lab coats. Nurses approach the workers with plates full of powder, which the workers snort through the silver straw. The workers go to waiting rooms, much like the "washroom" that CASSIUS entered. They transform almost magically into equisapiens.*)

STEVE LIFT: This is how we—

(*STEVE LIFT's voice is drowned out as CASSIUS flashes back to when he snorted the spiral line of powder on the Mr. Ed plate. Then we flash to a shot of the Equisapien who fell over in the washroom. And finally we cut back to a shot of the animated workers snorting powder and turning into equisapiens. The images flash over and over, faster and faster. CASSIUS hyperventilates. His eyes tear up.*)

CASSIUS: Wait. Hold up. Wait. Wait! What the fuck did you have me snort!?

(*CASSIUS jumps up. STEVE LIFT grabs the gun.*)

CASSIUS: Answer me, man! I'm not even high!

STEVE LIFT: You're not? What—

(CASSIUS *is in tears.*)

CASSIUS: (*Pointing to the gun*) Muthafucka—that shit don't scare me! If you gave me some mutation shit, I *want* you to shoot me!

STEVE LIFT: Cash. What you snorted was 100 percent Peruvian.

CASSIUS: Cocaine? It was coke?

STEVE LIFT: You heard what I said.

CASSIUS: You said, "100 percent Peruvian." Be precise. They got horses in Peru, probably.

STEVE LIFT: It was cocaine, man. I'm not evil. This ain't a movie. This is real life. I wouldn't just slip you the fusing catalyst. You don't feel high because your adrenaline is pumpin' so hard. You're harshin' your buzz.

(CASSIUS *slumps back into his seat.*)

STEVE LIFT: Okay, the proposal I was going to make was this: this new caliber of worker—they are bigger, stronger, and hopefully they don't gripe as much. Soon, there will be millions of them. They will be the future of industry.

CASSIUS: This is crazy, y—

STEVE LIFT: They'll develop their own identity and customs. They may wish to rebel, organize. We need someone to represent WorryFree's interests. Someone they can relate to.

CASSIUS: A manager—that's a man-horse.

STEVE LIFT: No. An Equisapien Martin Luther King. One that we control. One that we create. We want to frame the discussion. Give them a hero.

CASSIUS: So you want to con them into becoming monstrosities, work the shit out of them, and give them false hope by tricking them into following a leader who actually works for you?

STEVE LIFT: Basically. Keeps shit simple.

CASSIUS: But me? Why would you single out me?

STEVE LIFT: Cassius, you're amazing. You rose so quickly at Regalview. I need a man like you. Hungry. Not afraid to shank your friends if they get in the way. Look, you're freaked out. Ready to say no. Go home. Think about it. After looking at what I'm offering you.

(STEVE LIFT *hands Cassius a piece of paper that reads* I'M OFFERING YOU $100,000,000.)

CASSIUS: No amount is gonna make me wanna do that. Are you crazy?

STEVE LIFT: Two things. One: it would be only a five-year contract. After five years, we give you the Diffuser Antidote Special Sauce Serum and you're back to normal. Two: don't forget, you'd have a horse dick.

CASSIUS: Special Sauce Serum? You're making that up. It doesn't sound real.

STEVE LIFT: Oh, it's real. So's the offer. Five years as our man among horses. One hundred million dollars. Go home. Think about it. Holla at me later.

INTERIOR — CASSIUS'S CAR

CASSIUS sinks into the passenger seat of his own car as FANCY SUIT GUY drives. He looks contemplatively out the window while wiping his still-bleeding forehead.

INTERIOR — CASSIUS'S CHIC APARTMENT

Morning. CASSIUS is sleeping in his clothes from the night before. He tosses and turns, putting the pillow over his head to block the light. There is blood on the pillow. He has a flashback to STEVE LIFT's private office. We see STEVE LIFT and the mirror on the desk with the cocaine residue and straw. Then we see the Mr. Ed plate being pushed toward CASSIUS. CASSIUS wakes up frantically and grabs the piece of paper with the offer on it. There is a phone number for STEVE LIFT. A split screen shows STEVE LIFT in bed with two sleeping women.

STEVE LIFT: Cassius!

CASSIUS: Why'd you give me a different plate?

STEVE LIFT: Huh?

CASSIUS: Why'd you give me coke on a different plate? Yours was on a mirror.

STEVE LIFT: Was it? I don't know. I was high. Presentation?

CASSIUS: That seems—

STEVE LIFT: Dude. Why would I slip that to you without your knowledge? I thought you had an answer for me. I got all excited.

CASSIUS: I told you my answer: no.

(CASSIUS hangs up. He picks up a newspaper that's sitting on his nightstand. A column on the front page reads: PEOPLE SHOULD WORRY ABOUT WORRYFREE. *It's an article about the unethical conduct of WorryFree. The byline reads:* ERIC ARNOLD. CASSIUS *picks up the phone and dials.)*

VOICE ON PHONE: *San Francisco Chronicle.* Good morning.

CASSIUS: Eric Arnold, please.

ERIC: *(Offscreen)* Hello?

CASSIUS: *(Overdubbed by white actor)* Mr. Arnold. My name is Cassius Green. I've got some information about WorryFree that you will be very interested in.

ERIC: *(Offscreen)* Shoot.

CASSIUS: *(Overdubbed by a white actor)* Okay, they're making horse people. Half-horse, half-human workers. You snort this coke but it's not coke and you get big horse nostrils but you keep your feet and I might have unknowingly snorted—

ERIC: *(Offscreen, disbelieving)* Jake?

CASSIUS: *(Overdubbed by white actor)* No. Cassius. Cassius Green. This is bigger than Watergate—

ERIC: *(Offscreen)* Okay, WorryFree is making horse people. Well, this sounds very important. I'll have to hit you back in a few minutes.

CASSIUS: Aight, cool. Peace.

(CASSIUS hangs up. He turns on the TV and flips through channels. He stops at a morning talk show: The View. *Laughter.)*

WHOOPI GOLDBERG: . . . just can't get enough of these dang YouTubes! This next one got twenty-one million views and counting in one day! And it is a guilty pleasure! These big gorilla goons are helping these fancy suited guys break up a strike and—well, just watch!

(The YouTube video shows an attractive woman striker holding a Coca-Cola can up to the camera, shaking it vigorously, and smiling sweetly. Then she throws it with perfect form and great velocity. It goes past the Blackwater guards and hits CASSIUS *on the forehead. When the can hits there is a cartoonlike sound effect:* Boing!)

CASSIUS: Fuck!!!

CAN THROWER: Have a Coke and a smile, bitch!

(The video shows the CAN THROWER *smiling and taking a theatrical bow while fellow strikers clap. Roaring laughter from* The View's *studio audience.* WHOOPI GOLDBERG *is laughing uncontrollably.)*

WHOOPI GOLDBERG: Oh. My. God! Whoa! Can we get her on the show!? And she is pretty! Seriously—

*(*CASSIUS *turns off the TV. The phone rings.)*

CASSIUS: Hello, Mr. Arnold—

VOICE ON PHONE: *(Offscreen)* Mr. Green?

CASSIUS: Yes.

VOICE ON PHONE: *(Offscreen)* This is Dale Schillit from the Meyers-O'Hara firm. We saw the YouTube clip and we think we can turn your suffering into something serendipitous.

CASSIUS: You're a lawyer. You want me to sue? Who would—

(A spilt screen shows DALE SCHILLIT in a big executive's office with an amazing view.)

DALE SCHILLIT: Not a law firm. We're an ad firm developing campaigns for Coca-Cola. The clip is a post-media media phenomenon. We want to make an ad campaign that'll make you wealthy and famous.

CASSIUS: Apparently, I'm already famous.

DALE SCHILLIT: For being humiliated. We can turn this on its ear for you. We want to develop a multiyear campaign for Coca-Cola with you as the centerpiece.

CASSIUS: Then I'll be even more famous for being humiliated.

DALE SCHILLIT: But you'll be rich. So more people will respect you for turning this into an opportunity.

CASSIUS: Okay. No thanks.

DALE SCHILLIT: Don't answer too fast. This is my direct number I'm calling from. Hit me back if you change your mind.

CASSIUS: Aight, cool. Peace.

(CASSIUS realizes that he has been sketching a horse on the newspaper while talking. He jumps up, pats his pockets, and riffles through them.)

EXTERIOR — CITY STREET

CASSIUS is walking out of a mobile phone store and dialing on a cell phone. It's different from his old one. He walks briskly as he talks.

VOICE ON PHONE: *San Francisco Chronicle.* Good morning.

CASSIUS: *(Overdubbed by white actor)* Eric Arnold, please.

VOICE ON PHONE: Hold the line . . . He's not in. Do you want voicemail?

CASSIUS: (*Overdubbed by white actor*) Yes, please . . . Mr. Arnold, please return my call. I've left two other messages. I know it sounds crazy, but let me explain. Although I already did on my last message. Anyway, you have my home number—maybe you called me on that while I was out. I had to go buy a new cell phone because I guess I lost mine last night. My cell number is 510-555-8792.

INTERIOR — MEDICAL WAITING ROOM

CASSIUS sits in a waiting room, reading a National Enquirer. *The cover has a crudely Photoshopped picture of a person with the head of a horse. It does not look real at all. The headline reads:* HORSE PEOPLE STEALING JOBS FROM SLAVES! *The TV is blaring an episode from* Entertainment Tonight. *CASSIUS looks up at it.*

ENTERTAINMENT TONIGHT HOST: In the strangest thing to happen in entertainment or advertising history, the Coke-and-a-smile-bitch YouTube clip—which, as of noon today has gotten fifty-four million views in twenty-seven hours—has created an unlikely pairing. Coca-Cola has officially announced that they are in talks with Cynthia Rose, the beautiful, if foul-mouthed, heroine of the infamous clip. Coca-Cola will reportedly sign Rose to an advertising contract for an amount of money that would make most of us cry.

(The show cuts away to a press conference. DALE SCHILLIT is behind a podium with cameras flashing.)

DALE SCHILLIT: It's a new time in media. People think differently. We're staying ahead of the curve. People really connect with this clip. Cynthia's the new breed of pop star, and if everybody's gonna get their fifteen minutes of fame, we wanna be holding the stopwatch.

(Back to the Entertainment Tonight *studio.)*

ENTERTAINMENT TONIGHT HOST: The strike breaker who got hilariously pegged in that clip has been revealed to be named—

ENTERTAINMENT TONIGHT HOST AND RECEPTIONIST: Cassius Green!

INTERIOR — DOCTOR'S EXAMINATION ROOM

CASSIUS is standing in front of the doctor, facing him. He drops his pants.

DOCTOR: Looks normal to me.

CASSIUS: I was worried that it might be different. It . . . it seems bigger.

DOCTOR: Looks normal to me. Nothing extraordinary.

(CASSIUS pulls his pants up.)

CASSIUS: So . . . not like a horse?

(The DOCTOR is baffled.)

DOCTOR: What kind of drugs are you on?

EXTERIOR — CITY STREET

CASSIUS rushes down the street to his car, dialing on his phone. He puts it to his ear.

DETROIT: *(Offscreen)* Hello?

CASSIUS: I need to see you immediately. Please. It's important.

INTERIOR — CASSIUS'S CHIC APARTMENT

CASSIUS is standing in front of DETROIT, facing her. He starts unbuttoning his pants.

DETROIT: No, Cassius. Too soon.

CASSIUS: Not like that. Really. Tell me if it looks different.

(CASSIUS pulls his pants down. DETROIT looks.)

DETROIT: Looks the same to me. What am I looking for? Herpes or crabs or something? Did you go out and fuck some girl raw?

CASSIUS: No. It doesn't look bigger? 'Cause it feels bigger.

DETROIT: *(Laughing)* Well, I'm glad you're feelin' yourself! Is that why you kept trying to booty-call me last night?

CASSIUS: I didn't call you. I told you I lost my phone. I lost it at the party. I just got a new one today.

(DETROIT looks at her phone.)

DETROIT: I got a call from you at . . . 3:23 A.M. And a video message that I didn't check yet. I assumed it was lewd at that time of the morning.

CASSIUS: Can I see that?

(DETROIT hands the phone to CASSIUS. He presses play and they both watch. It's a video message from one of the equisapiens, who is apparently operating the phone while it's on the floor. There are other equisapiens shoving their heads into and out of frame.)

EQUISAPIEN: Help me! Please! I'm hurting!

(The equisapiens start whinnying and getting very excited. They are struggling against the chains that bind their legs and make it difficult to move.)

OTHER EQUISAPIENS: I'm hurting! Help me! I'm hurting! Please!

(The equisapiens get so excited that they kick the phone around. We see various body parts and a WorryFree logo on the wall. Then we see workers in WorryFree uniforms come in and inject the equisapiens with some kind of sedative. A more managerial-looking WorryFree worker punches a code into a wall-mounted dial pad, which loosens the chains of the now sedated equisapiens. With the chains slack, the equisapiens are able to walk again, and the workers herd them back into the stalls. The managerial-looking worker punches in another code, and the chains tighten once more. We then see STEVE LIFT walk in wearing a ridiculously colored bathrobe.)

STEVE LIFT: Quiet down, you motherfucking freaks of nature. I'm tryin' to get high. This is me time and you're—

(The video cuts off.)

DETROIT: What the fuck was that, Cassius!?

CASSIUS: I guess I found my phone. Baby, everything's crazy. I'm scared. This is why I called.

DETROIT: What does that have to do—

CASSIUS: Those things are called equisapiens. They are genetically modified human beings. WorryFree is on some Frankenstein shit. They are making a new species of worker that is more efficient than humans and easier to control. Who knows how many they've made already.

DETROIT: What the fuck!?

CASSIUS: That's what *I* said.

DETROIT: Oh my God. Oh shit. But . . . how were you—

CASSIUS: They want to create a leader for them. Someone the equisapiens look up to as a hero. One that WorryFree controls. They offered me the job.

DETROIT: I can't believe this shit. This doesn't seem real. We can't let them do this. There must be a way—

CASSIUS: I told them no. But I was worried that I may have snorted the activator or whatever.

DETROIT: People have to know about this, Cash. We—you have to tell them. (*Pointing toward CASSIUS's crotch*) But why did—

CASSIUS: I thought I was turning into a horse person. I thought I snorted the activator, but I guess it was just coke after all.

DETROIT: What? Well, why focus on your dick? From the video, they have those huge nostrils. You could have asked me to check your nostrils.

CASSIUS: Okay, are my nostrils bigger?

(*DETROIT checks. CASSIUS is unconsciously flaring his nostrils.*)

DETROIT: Yes, because you keep flaring them.

(*It becomes clear that CASSIUS is actually flaring his nostrils because he is breaking down from the stress and starting to cry. As he cries, DETROIT moves closer to console him.*)

INTERIOR — CASSIUS'S CHIC APARTMENT

Night. CASSIUS and DETROIT are lying in bed after having sex.

DETROIT: I just want you to know, I need to be clear: we're still not together, okay?

CASSIUS: Okay. And I just want you to know: I'm not going back. It's just wrong. I can't be a Power Caller anymore. I can't work for WorryFree . . . And I need you, D.

DETROIT: I think that's a great decision, Cassius. But I have to say that I still have problems with all this.

CASSIUS: But now I'm —

DETROIT: You quitting now won't get applause from me. You happily sold slaves and bombs and scabbed against the strike. It was only something happening to you—your own self-interest—that made you go against them.

CASSIUS: Isn't that how we all make decisions? And I didn't—

DETROIT: No. It doesn't have to be.

CASSIUS: Plus, I see myself in their eyes: WorryFree and Regalview. To them, I'm this most-likely-to-sell-out asshole that they can manipulate. And they're right. But I'm not gonna continue to be that dude.

DETROIT: Good for you, Cash. But that doesn't change what I said about us . . . Also, I kind of messed with somebody last night.

CASSIUS: What does "kind of messed with" mean? Did you—

DETROIT: We did "everything but."

CASSIUS: "Everything but"!? You know that can be way nastier than just . . . What exactly . . . Did you—

(*DETROIT nods.*)

CASSIUS: Did he—

(*DETROIT smiles and nods.*)

CASSIUS: (*Doing some unintelligible hand gyration*) Did you both—

DETROIT: (*Nodding*) Cassius, we were broken up. We *are* broken up. It's you and I who shouldn't be messing around. Don't you want to know who it was?

CASSIUS: Well, are you planning on fucking him, or everything-but-ing with him, again?

DETROIT: No.

CASSIUS: Then I don't want to know. I mean, I think I know. Was it . . . No, I don't wanna know.

(*CASSIUS reaches over and turns out the light. He dreams a rapid-fire montage of horses running, having sex, eating, pulling carriages. All of a sudden he is pulling the carriage and DIANA DEBAUCHERY is holding the reins.*)

DIANA: This is where the magic happens, Gigolo!

(*CASSIUS wakes up, breathing heavily. He looks toward DETROIT, but she is gone.*)

EXTERIOR — STREET

It's nighttime in a business district. DETROIT and twenty other people, mainly women, are running full bore down the street, laughing and whooping. They are all wearing black, and they each have one black grease stripe under their left eye. Many are carrying bags. They run to a parked van that is waiting for them. The van doors fly open and the group starts filing in. DETROIT pauses before she jumps in, looking back at what they've accomplished.

DETROIT: It's a masterpiece.

SAMIYAH: Come on! You can come look at it later!

(*DETROIT jumps into the van, which pulls away.*)

Morning. DETROIT *is walking where she was the night before—only this time in the opposite direction. She has a huge smile on her face and has changed clothes. A crowd is gathering and looking at something. Some people are taking pictures. Many look bewildered. They are looking at a twenty-by-fifty-foot painted-wood-plank-and-cardboard sculpture of* STEVE LIFT *in a suit with his pants down, mating with a horse from behind. There are three-foot-high three-dimensional letters on the ground in front of the sculpture, which read:* WORRYFREE IS TURNING WORKERS INTO HORSES AND FUCKING THEM. DETROIT *listens to onlookers.*

MAN IN CROWD: (*To wife*) I have absolutely no idea what this is about.

(*The wife laughs.*)

OTHER MAN IN CROWD: Maybe the artist is saying that capitalism dehumanizes, and that capitalists are impelled by a desire to subjugate—no matter the human toll—like rapists who are driven to copulate.

DETROIT: Or maybe the artist is being literal. Maybe WorryFree is turning workers into horses. Literally.

OTHER MAN IN CROWD: And literally having sex with them?

(*DETROIT doesn't answer, but instead gazes at her work, satisfied. Her right earring reads* TELL HOMELAND SECURITY *and her left earring reads* WE ARE THE BOMB *in big block letters.*)

WOMAN IN CROWD: (*Offscreen*) What the hell!?

TEENAGE GIRL IN CROWD: (*Offscreen*) I don't get it.

EXTERIOR — TACO TRUCK

It's daytime. CASSIUS *looks over the taco truck menu. A* CAR AFICIONADO *is showing off his customized car to a friend.*

CASSIUS: (*To taco truck worker*) Three carne asada tacos and two al pastor.

(CASSIUS *waits for his order. The* CAR AFICIONADO *pops his trunk to show off what's inside. There are woofers and a giant flat-screen TV that pops up.*)

CAR AFICIONADO: I'ma be killin' 'em at the sideshow! I get internet, too. In case I wanna pull off the road and Facebook and shit.

(*The* CAR AFICIONADO *plays a YouTube music clip, but stops it after a few seconds.*)

CAR AFICIONADO: Ay. You seen this shit? It'll have you rollin'.

(*He plays the clip of* CASSIUS *getting pegged by the Coke can. View counter: 110* MILLION VIEWS. *He and his friend explode in laughter.*)

CAR AFICIONADO: Damn, man! He's a mark!

CAR AFICIONADO'S FRIEND: Have a Coke and a smile, bitch! Ay, the broad that hit him is fine as hell, tho! Ay, click on that one.

(*They click on a clip titled "Look Like the Coke-and-a-Smile-Bitch Guy for Halloween." The clip shows a white middle-aged woman cutting a diagonal corner out of a Coke can, stapling it to an Afro wig, and putting it on.*)

WOMAN IN CLIP: Voilà! Just add some fake blood with face paint or lipstick and you're good.

CAR AFICIONADO: Now I know what my costume is gon' be for Halloween. But I'ma wear one of them loud-ass suits, too!

(*CASSIUS sneaks away without his tacos so he can avoid being noticed by the* CAR AFICIONADO *and the* CAR AFICIONADO'S FRIEND.)

EXTERIOR — STREET

CASSIUS walks down the street, sulking with his hands in his pockets, looking at the ground, kicking rocks and other things as he walks. CASSIUS's phone rings while he's walking past a WorryFree billboard that shows a happy family in a WorryFree housing unit.

CASSIUS: Hello?

VOICE ON PHONE: Hi! May I speak to Cassius Green, please?

CASSIUS: This is he.

VOICE ON PHONE: Mr. Green, my name is Doug Urgravé. I'm the producer of *Good Morning America*. We'd love to get you on our show later this week. To tell your side of the story.

(Silence.)

DOUG URGRAVÉ: Hello?

CASSIUS: You wanna make fun of me. I need to get off the phone right now. Sorry. I'll have to call you back.

(*CASSIUS walks until he gets to the corner and waits for the light to change, still sulking. A PASSENGER in a car that's also waiting for the light stares at him.*)

PASSENGER: Hey, aren't you that dude from the YouTube clip?

CASSIUS: Naw, man. Damn. Everybody thinks I'm him, but I—

(CASSIUS is hit in the chest with a large plastic cup of water that explodes all over him upon impact.)

PASSENGER: Sorry, all I have is water—

(Car peels off with an angry CASSIUS chasing it.)

PASSENGER: —it's healthier!

(The driver and the passenger are laughing with delight. CASSIUS keeps up with the car for a few seconds, but it gets away. He makes one last effort to swipe at it and falls over in the process. He gets up, snorts out while catching his breath, and shakes some dust off—like a horse. Then he walks to a nearby park. He looks terrible: he's still bleeding from the bandage and his clothes are dusty from the fall. He sits on a bench and stares out at nothing for hours, until the sun goes down.)

INTERIOR—CASSIUS'S CHIC APARTMENT

CASSIUS walks in his front door and starts dialing.

CASSIUS: Hey, Detroit. Can you load that video message from your phone to your computer? Send it to my phone, too. I have a plan.

INTERIOR—DINER

Morning. CASSIUS is sitting at a table. He's wearing a vintage leather aviator's cap and flight goggles to disguise himself. SALVADOR, SQUEEZE, and MIKE walk in and head toward CASSIUS, who smiles. They sit down.

SALVADOR: Don't say it.

CASSIUS: C'mon, man. It's the first time in my life that it's actually appropriate.

SALVADOR: Okay, whatever.

CASSIUS: I guess you're all wondering why I've called this meeting.

SALVADOR: It's either to announce that you're secretly the Red Baron or that we should drop everything and go to Burning Man.

CASSIUS: Shut up, man. It's all I could find. Everybody's fuckin' with me.

SQUEEZE: (*Sincerely*) How's that head wound?

CASSIUS: I think it's finally starting to close up. Look, I realize I've been an asshole—

SQUEEZE: A scab.

MIKE: A traitor.

SALVADOR: A scalawag.

CASSIUS: A what?

SALVADOR: A scalawag . . . you know, like a scoundrel.

CASSIUS: Scalawag sounds like something Popeye would say. And "scoundrel"? Are you going to challenge me to a duel or something?

SQUEEZE: Way off topic here.

CASSIUS: I'm sorry I let you all down. You may not ever want to be my friends again. I accept that. I was selfish and shortsighted. All I can do is do it right from now on. I think I'm in a position right now where I could really help the strike and help the union.

SQUEEZE: That's what I said a few days ago.

CASSIUS: Right. But it's about how we do it. And I've got a plan—

(A group of schoolchildren—led by their teachers—walks by the diner window. It's Halloween, and the kids are parading in their costumes. Eighty percent of them have CASSIUS *costumes: Afro wigs with Coke cans and fake blood attached.* CASSIUS, SQUEEZE, MIKE, *and* SALVADOR *are taken aback.)*

CASSIUS: What the hell!? It's only been three days! Fuck the internet!

EXTERIOR — STREET

CASSIUS drives his car to the park where the football players are playing. He gets out and runs toward them. They stop what they're doing to greet him.

EXTERIOR — STEVE LIFT'S MANSION

CASSIUS is dressed in a custodial uniform. He approaches a security-box dial pad outside a side gate at the mansion. He looks at his phone and plays the equisapiens' video message: the part where the manager is dialing a code. CASSIUS dials the same code and the gate opens. He walks in.

EXTERIOR — GALLERY

It's dusk. CASSIUS has just loaded the last of eight statues onto a flatbed rental truck. DETROIT is helping. They hug each other. The street is filled with kids carrying trick-or-treat bags and wearing Coke-and-a-smile-bitch Halloween costumes. One group of kids spots CASSIUS and starts throwing their Halloween candy at him. He runs to the other side of the truck, but the kids laugh and chase him. CASSIUS pleads to the adult of the group.

CASSIUS: C'mon, man! You gonna let 'em just do that?

(The adult reins in the kids.)

ADULT HALLOWEEN CHAPERONE: C'mon, y'all.

DETROIT: *(To CASSIUS, gesturing toward statues)* Are you sure this is gonna work?

CASSIUS: Not at all. But this is for part two of the plan. Tomorrow is part one.

EXTERIOR — AIRPORT

An airplane takes off.

EXTERIOR — NEW YORK CITY

CASSIUS is in a cab, looking out at the buildings in wonder. He has never been to New York. A street performer running a three-card Monte table is wearing a Coke-and-a-smile-bitch wig. Later, CASSIUS sees a homeless person wearing one.

INTERIOR — TV STUDIO CONTROL ROOM

Close-up on a video monitor. The monitor is playing a commercial with high pro-duction values. A jingle plays as we see a beautifully made-up CYNTHIA ROSE in very fashionable faux-anarchist attire. She is smiling into the camera with her hair blowing wildly, in slow motion, while a demonstration unfolds in the background. CYNTHIA ROSE reaches into her backpack and pulls out a Coca-Cola can, which seems to be glowing. Still smiling into the camera, she winks and throws the can at the head of an actor who looks very similar to CASSIUS. When it hits his head, the whole crowd—demonstrators, fellow suits, CYNTHIA ROSE, and Blackwater security—

starts singing "Have a Coke and a smile, bitch," Broadway musical–style, while dancing. The wounded FAKE CASSIUS—*who has been knocked to the ground—gets up, sips the Coke enthusiastically, and makes out wildly with* CYNTHIA ROSE. *As the thirty-second commercial ends, we pull back and see the busy control room.*

PRODUCER: Three, two, one: Camera One, go!

INTERIOR — TV STUDIO SOUNDSTAGE

We are on the set of I Got the S#*@ Kicked Outta Me!

GAME SHOW AUDIENCE: I Got the S#*@ Kicked Outta Me!

MARY RICH: I'm Mary Rich, and have we got a treat for you! Today on *I Got the S#*@ Kicked Outta Me*, YouTube sensation Cassius Green is here. Cassius, five hundred million views—

CASSIUS: Yeah, it's been crazy—

MARY RICH: Five hundred million people have watched you get pegged in the noggin and be utterly humiliated. It's effin' hilarious. Cassius, what say you?

CASSIUS: Well, Mary, it is humiliating—

MARY RICH: Yet hilarious. The way your hand goes up really fast like that after the can bounces off your head . . . it has people ROFL-ing all over the world! You haven't made any previous public appearances, but you're here on this show now: Tell the audience why.

CASSIUS: I've got a new clip that I'm in—and an announcement. I only agreed to come on your show as a contestant in exchange for you guys playing the clip to your 150 million viewers.

MARY RICH: Well, if you want some ass, you gotta bring some ass! Get out there, and then we'll play your clip!

(We see a montage of CASSIUS *running through a gauntlet; being hit by paddles, having baseballs hurled at him, being assaulted by five kickboxers who are standing around him in a circle, and having sludgelike cow shit dumped on him. Afterward,* CASSIUS *is standing next to* MARY RICH. *He is totally covered in cow shit, except for his eyes.)*

CASSIUS: I'd like to play the clip now.

MARY RICH: Okay! Is it as crazy as the Coke-and-a-smile-bitch clip? It couldn't possibly be.

CASSIUS: It's crazier, Mary.

MARY RICH: Woo-hoo! Let's roll the clip!

(The clip plays. It's the video message that the equisapiens sent to DETROIT.*)*

MARY RICH: Well, that wasn't funny. It was just weird and scary.

CASSIUS: Mary, as a Power Caller for Regalview, one of my clients was WorryFree. This video is incontrovertible proof of WorryFree's evil programs! They are changing humans into these grotesque horse people! I want the world to know that they are manipulating humanity for the sake of profit!

MARY RICH: Okay, what would you like everyone to do?

CASSIUS: I don't know. Call their congressmen?

INTERIOR — BAR

CASSIUS sits in a booth, reading a newspaper. SQUEEZE walks in and sits down.

SQUEEZE: How's that revolutionary new beg-your-congressman thing going?

CASSIUS: It's not. I mean people have called, but nothing's happening. Man, I expected that once the world saw that video, once everyone knew, they'd have to do something. But I guess nobody really cares.

SQUEEZE: It's not that people don't care. People think that there's nothing they can do. We have to show them. Look, if Mike Tyson came in here and wanted to beat your ass—

CASSIUS: How come everybody uses Mike as a hypothetical? "What if Mike Tyson wanted to fight you?" "How much money would you need to fight Mike Tyson?" "What if Mike Tyson was tryna holla at your girl?" Nobody ever says "What if Dick Cheney wanted you dead?" or "What if the CIA or the Chicago police was torturing you?" People need to lay off—

SQUEEZE: Anyway, if Mike Tyson came in here and wanted to beat your ass, you might know that the only way to stop him is to knock him out, but knowing that ain't enough. If you don't know *how* to knock him out, you're gonna feel powerless and either run or take an ass beating.

CASSIUS: And die.

SQUEEZE: Yeah. So that's why the next part of your plan is really important. Tomorrow, we fly.

CASSIUS: But if you're drunk, you might think you can beat Mike Tyson. Maybe everybody just needs to get drunk.

SQUEEZE: No. You're fucking up my analogy.

Once again, we see a strike in which the strikers are violently and successfully keeping out the scabs. All of the strikers are wearing Coke-and-a-smile-bitch wigs. A TV news crew is on the scene.

TV NEWS REPORTER: We can't explain why all of the strikers here at Regalview are dressed up in their Coke-and-a-smile-bitch wigs, which are supposed to mimic—or mock—the now infamous Cassius Green. We can't tell you because none of the strikers will tell us why. We see the Blackwater security guards forming their perimeter around the Power Callers. All of the Power Callers are there, except for Cassius. Although the strikers have been extremely militant over the past six weeks, they have not been able to stop the juggernaut of Blackwater guards from breaking through the line.

BLACKWATER AGENT: Hut! Hut! Go!

(The Blackwater security guards are pushing through a massive sea of strikers dressed in Coke-and-a-smile-bitch wigs. They are meeting some resistance, but pushing strikers to the left and right with relative ease and trampling over many as they build up speed. There seems to be no stopping them as they head toward the door. Then we hear a whistle blow loudly. One group of strikers jumps quickly to the side, revealing a stoic group of strikers who aren't moving and—BLAM! the Blackwater guards bang their heads into these stoic strikers and fall backward. We see that this last group were not strikers: they were DETROIT's statues dressed in clothes and Coke-and-a-smile-bitch wigs. The crowd cheers wildly! The Blackwater guards and Power Callers get up, disheveled, some of them more confused than others.)

BLACKWATER AGENT: Go around, soldiers! Clockwise! No retreat!

(Cassius, in a Coke-and-a-smile-bitch wig, stands on the shoulders of the statues and loudly blows a whistle. On both sides of the Blackwater guards, the strikers jump out of the way and we see two groups of very large people wearing Coke-and-

a-smile-bitch wigs: it's the football team. They are running toward the Blackwater guards. They have custom wigs over their helmets and jackets over their pads. They smash into the group: KABLAM! SMASH! THUD!)

TV NEWS REPORTER: Eew.

(The crowd cheers even more wildly! The Blackwater guards are on the ground in various states of consciousness and mobility. Many of the Power Callers crawl away; some continue to lie there in pain. It seems the strikers have won this bout.)

TV NEWS REPORTER: Somebody get that ambulance over here!

(CASSIUS snatches his own wig off and whoops and hollers, hugging SAL, SQUEEZE, and MIKE.)

TV NEWS REPORTER: Apparently, Cassius Green, former Power Caller, has switched sides, and is involved in the calamity that we just witnessed. Jan, can we play that back for our viewers that—

(Three large UPS/SWAT-looking trucks pull up very quickly, and dozens of Blackwater security guards pile out of each truck.)

BLACKWATER GUARDS: Hut! Hut! Hut! Hut!

TV NEWS REPORTER: Looks like the cavalry has arrived, folks!

(Blackwater guards in riot gear force their way through the crowd, bashing people in the head with batons, screaming as if going to war. Wigs are flying everywhere. People are bloody. CASSIUS, SAL, and SQUEEZE look stunned and frightened by this show of force. They look defeated. Then CASSIUS pulls out his phone and dials.)

CASSIUS: *(To SAL and SQUEEZE)* This is where the magic happens.

(CASSIUS blows the whistle loudly into the phone. The whistle goes on for many seconds. CASSIUS stares down the street, past the commotion of protesters in wigs being

beaten bloody and senseless. We hear a rumbling that gets louder until the vibrations are shaking the surrounding windows and cars. The TV news van and Blackwater trucks are shaking as if there's an earthquake. A Blackwater guard looks down the street in disbelief. It's an equisapien stampede. About one hundred equisapiens are galloping on all fours toward the melee, whinnying, neighing, snorting, and trampling everything in their path: cars, trash cans, etc. Their muscles are rippling and their hair is blowing as they run. Some of the Regalview strikers look terrified.)

RANDOM REGALVIEW STRIKER: (*Scared*) Oh shit.

CASSIUS: (*Through bullhorn*) Strikers! These are our friends! They're on our side!

(The driver of one of the Blackwater trucks attempts to ram the equisapiens at high speed, but the equisapiens part like the Red Sea to avoid it. One particularly large equisapien stays in the middle of the street and charges the truck. At the last second, the equisapien jumps to his right and, standing sideways on his hind legs, punches through the driver's-side window and snatches the driver out. The truck careens out of control and crashes into a building. After this we see a shot of a protester in a Coke-and-a-smile-bitch wig getting beaten by a Blackwater agent. The Blackwater agent is grabbed from behind by a towering female equisapien who throws him several feet. The agent gets up and scurries away. The equisapien reaches out to shake the hand of the grateful yet spooked protester, who pets her hand instead of shaking it. The equi-sapien snorts. Elsewhere, equisapiens and Blackwater agents are in full brawl. Some equisapiens are on their hind legs, fighting in a traditional boxing style. Others are on all fours, ramming the parked Blackwater trucks with the broad side of their backs. One equisapien gets tasered. It is clear that the equisapiens have the upper hand and are about to help the Regalview callers win the skirmish. In the middle of the melee, which is dying down, one equisapien walks on all fours toward CASSIUS. We can see that this is the same equisapien whom CASSIUS first met in the stall, GUY IN STALL.)

CASSIUS: (*Speaking loudly and slowly, as if talking to an alien*) THANK. YOU. WE. ARE HONORED. BY YOUR. PRESENCE.

GUY IN STALL: C'mon, dude. I grew up in East Oakland. I can understand you if you talk regular. My name is DeMarius.

CASSIUS: Oh, hey. Cassius. Cassius Green.

(CASSIUS and DEMARIUS give each other a fist bump. We see a group of five Blackwater agents creeping slowly into the frame, behind DEMARIUS. The Blackwater agents have their batons out, ready to strike. They are moving cautiously, one step at a time, close together, in a forward-facing huddle. Without turning his head away from CASSIUS, DEMARIUS firmly plants his hands/forefeet on the ground and gives a swift and powerful horse kick to the agents, knocking them all down, leaving some unconscious and others crawling away. DEMARIUS stands on his hind legs, looks at the group that he kicked, and lets out a loud whinny. He then surveys the rest of the scene. Many of the Blackwater agents are running away, and so are the Power Callers. It looks like a real victory for the strikers this time. In the distance, DEMARIUS sees a helicopter with guns approaching. DEMARIUS turns back toward CASSIUS. SQUEEZE is now standing next to him.)

SQUEEZE: (To DEMARIUS) Same struggle. Same fight.

(SQUEEZE and DEMARIUS do a clenched-fist salute, with CASSIUS joining in at the last second.)

GUY IN STALL: (In a booming voice, louder than a bullhorn) Equisapiens! We're done! Move out!

(The equisapiens gallop away down the street and around the corner as the crowd of strikers cheers. The helicopter follows the equisapiens. The applause and cheers for the equisapiens turns into a victory celebration for the strikers. Someone in a Coke-and-a-smile-bitch wig comes up and taps CASSIUS on the back. He turns and we see that it's DETROIT. They smile hugely at each other.)

DETROIT: I need to talk to the brilliant mastermind-slash-hero of the day. Slash-important-deed-doer . . . Slash-kiss-me.

(CASSIUS blows the whistle and grabs DETROIT. *They kiss and embrace as the strike continues behind them, complete with a police melee.)*

EXTERIOR — STREET

CASSIUS's black Mercedes-Benz cruises down the street and pulls up in front of the garage-door entrance to CASSIUS's *old studio apartment.*

EXTERIOR — CASSIUS'S STUDIO APARTMENT

CASSIUS walks up to the Benz and we realize that it wasn't him driving. The driver gets out with the car still running. It's SALVADOR. *He's smiling.*

SALVADOR: Man, are you serious?

CASSIUS: Serious as cake in a can.

SALVADOR: Hell yeah! That's serious! You're givin'—

CASSIUS: Hey, it's yours. I have a car that'll do me just fine to get to work at Regalview.

(CASSIUS gestures toward a small used sedan.)

CASSIUS: Plus, I wanted to say sorry.

SALVADOR: Just sayin' "sorry" woulda been fine. But I don't wanna insult you. I'll take it!

(SALVADOR and CASSIUS exchange a one-handed man hug and SALVADOR walks back to get in the car.)

SALVADOR: Now that the strike's won, you're okay with coming back to work with us at Regalview as a lowly, *regular* telemarketer?

CASSIUS: Yep. Even though Regalview Power Callers are still doing their evil shit and WorryFree is still turning humans into grotesque horse people for profit, we have to hold our ground somewhere. Also, I need a job.

SALVADOR: Okay, man. Consider yourself a member of the new and glorious Telemarketers Union then!

(SAL *smiles and gets into the car.* DETROIT *approaches as* CASSIUS *walks toward the garage door. She is wearing earrings that say* BELLA CIAO *in big block letters on both sides.*)

DETROIT: So, what about being part of something important?

CASSIUS: I *am* part of something important. And not just something: it's the right thing. We're all a part of something. It's the choices we make to sacrifice for something greater than ourselves that actually matters later on.

DETROIT: They matter even after the sun explodes?

CASSIUS: *Especially* after the sun explodes.

(CASSIUS *reaches down and pulls the garage door open. It's his same old studio apartment, but now it's decked out like a stylish, luxurious apartment, with recessed lights and expensive furniture. It's fly. The man in the framed picture looks prouder than ever.* CASSIUS *looks at* DETROIT.)

CASSIUS: Well, I couldn't come back to the exact same place after living like that, could I?

(DETROIT *smiles. She is not judging. They walk in.* CASSIUS *struggles to pull the door shut.*)

CASSIUS: Thought I fixed—

(The door slams down hard, smashing CASSIUS *in the nose. He covers his face and screams.* DETROIT *runs to him.)*

CASSIUS: Fuck! Why the—

*(*CASSIUS*'s cussing turns into a loud whinny.* DETROIT *is startled.)*

DETROIT: What the—

*(*CASSIUS*'s hands come off of his face. He has gigantic nostrils and large eyes. He's snorting and confused. He is turning into an equisapien.* DETROIT *screams. Cut to black.)*

I'd like to thank all the folks who gave me helpful critiques and encouragement as I was writing and re-writing this screenplay.

Vanessa Carlisle, Raj Patel, Oliver Stone and staff, Jeremy Glick, Stephen Marshall, Gayatri Roshan, Ted Hope, David Cross, W. Kamau Bell, Patton Oswalt, Alex Rivera, Dave Eggers, and Daniel Gumbiner.

I owe you all a drink or dinner at a place that's not too expensive. Unless we're gonna share an order or something. Not all at the same time. Catch me when I've got some cash on me.

BOOTS RILEY lives in Oakland, California. He is the frontman and song-writer for The Coup. Right-wing columnist and Fox News contributor Michelle Malkin once called his work "A stomach-turning example of anti-Americanism disguised as high-brow intellectualism." Boots was surprised and elated by the compliment.